[Gabe]

[Gabe]

a novella

Gary Soto

STEPHEN F. AUSTIN STATE UNIVERISTY PRESS

Copyright © 2019 Gary Soto

All rights reserved. For information about permission to reproduce selections from this book write to Permissions:

Stephen F. Austin State University Press
PO Box 13007, SFA Station
Nacogdoches, TX 75962
sfapress@sfasu.edu
936-468-1078

For information about special discounts for bulk purchases, please contact:

Texas A&M University Press Consortium
tamupress.com

ISBN: 978-1-62288-541-1

In Memory of Papa Mike

Founder of Fresno's Poverello House

As Gabe Mendoza approached the downtown library, miserably sweaty, he scolded himself for forgetting his baseball cap at home. The afternoon was hot, maddening hot. He stopped under a tree and spied the temperature on the corner bank building: 104. Through the wavering heat, he eyed a figure in a 49ers sweatshirt. Dang, Gabe thought. What's wrong with this guy? A sweatshirt in this heat?

"Son," the figure beckoned to him.

Son? Gabe wondered. Was this homeless man looking for a handout?

"It's me, your dad." The figure in dirty clothes was pulling a large suitcase on wheels. The man did his best to hoist a smile.

The vagrant did resemble his dad, whom Gabe hadn't seen in four years. His dad had driven away in the family's best car, with his clothes and the household computer in the backseat. He had also loaded the car with cases of soda and bottled water, as if he were thirsty for a life other than the one he had with them.

In truth, Gabe had been relieved when he disappeared. His parents had begun to argue a lot, their heated voices vibrating through the bedroom walls. He had been eight at the time, and nervous that his dad might hit his mother. How he had feared those evenings when his dad sat in his recliner, drinking in front of a blaring television.

"Son," the man repeated, with a smile that revealed a missing tooth. "It's me, Gabe, your father! I'm back in town."

A lump rose in Gabe's throat when the man had called him by name. He took a step back and shaded his eyes from the hurtful sun. He had to focus on the man to make sure it was his dad.

"I don't know you," Gabe said flatly. He was disgusted by the man's dirty neck. And that worn and faded sweatshirt? It looked like the kind of thing a dog would sleep on.

Gabe's dad shook his head. His forehead was carved with lines of a hard life. "So this is how your mother's raising you?"

"None of your business how she's raising me," Gabe replied. "I don't know you, mister."

The man's tone changed. "Aw, come on, Gabriel…"

Gabe ignored his dad's plea and hurried toward the entrance of the library, his head down. He was confused. Why was his dad here? Then he remembered that the Poverello House, a sanctuary for the homeless, was only five blocks away, and that the destitute ghosted nearby until the doors opened for prayer and dinner. His dad was one of them now, a dirty ghost from his childhood.

[Gabe]

"I'm your old man," the man called after him. "Show some respect."

Gabe struggled to keep from turning and shouting that he was nothing but a bum. He gripped the handle of the heavy glass door, greased by hundreds of sweaty palms, and entered the library. He didn't glance back as he moved quickly past the foyer into the main reading area.

I'm safe, Gabe thought. I'm inside.

A vision of his mother rose momentarily, and he held her in his heart—she was the true parent. She worked as a cashier at Walmart, where all day her fingers touched money, checks, and debit and credit cards, none of which belonged to her. She worked long hours, and at the end of her eight-hour shift her ankles hurt. How long could a person stand in one spot without falling over?

"He's homeless," Gabe whispered to himself. Everything he owned was stuffed in that suitcase on wheels, which he hauled like a donkey pulling a cart.

In the magazine alcove, Gabe discovered that each of the four chairs was occupied by an old man. At their sides lay bulging plastic bags and backpacks, a sign that they were transients. Gabe could smell them. He wondered if they were deadbeat fathers, too.

When Gabe got home, he found his mother lying on the couch. A washcloth filled with ice cubes lay on her round stomach. Her furry pink slippers, which resembled balls of cotton candy, had slipped off her feet.

"Hi, Mom," Gabe said. He pulled at the front of his shirt, which was plastered damply to his chest. His cheeks were nearly as pink as his mother's slippers.

She turned her red face to him, smiled weakly, and rose to a sitting position. "Is this global warming?" she asked.

Gabe ignored her question. He decided to be direct.

"I saw him," he began. He walked toward the recliner, the centerpiece of their living room, and sat down.

"Who?" she asked.

"Dad."

"Your father?" Seconds ago, his mom had worn a sleepy expression, but now she was wide awake.

Gabe nodded.

She sat up straighter on the couch. "Where?" she asked

"The library," Gabe answered. He gazed briefly at the muted television. The actors were throwing their hands up in the air and shouting at each other. A soap opera.

"How did he look?" she inquired.

[Gabe]

"Homeless," Gabe answered. He told her about the suitcase, and his dirty clothes.

"I bet you it's the one he took when he left us."

Over a two-month period before his dad had vanished, he'd stolen things from their house to keep himself in whiskey and beer. There had been another woman as well, if the lipstick on the collar of a dress shirt was any indication.

"If he dares to show up here, I'm calling the cops," his mother warned. She pushed her weight from the couch, kicked her slippers out of the way, and headed for the telephone in the hallway. "No," she reconsidered, "I'm going to call Jerry now."

Jerry was one of her two brothers. The other was Mathew, who lived alone on a plot of land in the foothills. Uncle Jerry had been a cop who patrolled the rural roads of Tulare County, but his career had ended when he injured his back— and not from breaking up a street fight but from moving a refrigerator for his girlfriend. Now Uncle Jerry delivered breads and cakes, but he was no squeezable loaf of softness. He was hard as iron, no one to fool with.

"Don't, Mom," Gabe pleaded. "Don't call him." He was scared that his uncle would grab his dad in a headlock and walk him into a wall. His dad was already hurting; he didn't need further punishment.

But his mother was deaf to his plea. She picked up the phone and made the call.

"Whatever," Gabe mumbled and went into the kitchen, where he poured himself a glass of Gatorade. He took the glass and went outside through the kitchen door.

In the backyard, the afternoon sun sparkled off the aluminum pie tins they had strung up over their rows of tomato plants. The pie tins weren't intended to keep tomato-loving birds away, however. They were there to alert Gabe and his mom whenever intruders scaled their fence along the alley. Over the past few weeks, he and his mother had discovered that the homeless were raiding their garden. When he heard the pie tins rattling like wind chimes, Gabe would hurry outside, clapping his hands and yelling, "Get out! This is our place, not yours." Embarrassed, most would drop what was in their hands and, sad as old dogs, leave without a whimper. Sometimes, touched by their poverty, Gabe would say, "Take a few. It's OK." He would pick the tomatoes off the vine and press them into their cupped hands.

Gabe rattled the ice cubes in his tall glass and sized up the yard. The flowerbed that ran along the garage was scraggly with weeds, and the dazed zinnias needed water. He picked up the baseball bat lying in the weeds and brought it to his shoulder. He played softball at Holmes Playground, in a league for those kids who didn't possess the muscle or grit for the Babe Ruth League. At first, Gabe had considered his teammates scrubs, second-

[Gabe]

raters, losers even, but he admonished himself for those thoughts. He was conscious that most of his teammates couldn't afford uniforms and cleats, or bats and gloves, or the insurance required to join the Babe Ruth League teams. Plus, their families were unwilling or unable to drive their sons across town. Gas was expensive, time too precious.

Gabe swung the bat and imagined a softball sailing over the second baseman's head—no, farther, over the center fielder. When a pie tin began to rattle, he let the bat slide from his hands, no longer in his dream world of singles and doubles. He expected to see his father, scrawny as a scarecrow, standing among the tomatoes.

Had he really seen his father in front of the library? Or was the figure a mirage in the Fresno heat?

Gabe's mother threatened to file a restraining order at City Hall. "I'll do it tomorrow." Her eyes were leveled on the television, which was off—why watch a soap opera when you can create your own melodrama? She had a miserable, faraway expression. Her eyes lifted to the clock on the wall. It was 4:30pm.

Gabe left the living room. In his bedroom, he devoured a bag of barbecue pork rinds, then fell asleep with a small fan whirring at the end of his bed. He woke up with a sticky neck, the collar of his T-shirt dark with sweat. From the shadows on the wall, he guessed that it was near six o'clock. He sat on the bed's edge, head down and groggy.

"Let's go," he told his body, then forced himself to stand up. He washed his face, drank a glass of cold water, and got his bike from the garage.

Twenty minutes later, he arrived at the playground. He leaned his bike against the dugout, secured it with a lock, grabbed his mitt from the handlebars, and hustled to the infield. At first, he was grateful for his late arrival, since most of his teammates were bent over, panting. Coach Rodriguez had made them run wind sprints.

"Sorry, Coach," Gabe apologized. He popped his fist into the pocket of his glove, a sign that he was ready to play. "Where do you want me?"

"You're late, Mendoza," scolded the coach, an ex-marine. He turned and yelled, "Pablo, get over here! You're late, too." Coach Rodriguez instructed both boys to run to the other baseball diamond across the field and back. And to run, not jog or walk.

Pablo, a friend from school, was the real athlete on the team. Pablo could blast home runs, snag line drives, and slide into base with his eyes wide open. He was skillful and fearless.

As the two ran side by side, Gabe glanced

[Gabe]

enviously at Pablo. He was not only good at sports but also a straight-A student; he'd even once won a schoolwide spelling bee. Pablo had brainpower between his ears. After Gabe had done poorly on a sixth-grade vocabulary text, Pablo informed him, in private, that an ignoramus was not an extinct dinosaur.

Besides smarts—Gabe swallowed this bitter truth like aspirin—Pablo had another gift. Girls liked him. They liked him a lot. He had only to say "Hi," and the girls would giggle with excitement.

While they jogged, Gabe rummaged through his memory. He had to admit that he'd never had a girlfriend, unless he could count Rebecca Garcia. In fifth grade, she had filled her mouth with water from the drinking fountain and splashed it onto his shoes. The rumor was that she liked him. But at the time, he'd been far more interested in soccer than in girls.

As he and Pablo reached the far baseball diamond, Gabe heard a voice calling, "Son." He scanned the empty bleachers, then looked into the dugout, which was littered with cups, Popsicle sticks, and candy wrappers. His dad stood there alone, waving at him.

"Gabe," his dad called. *"Mi'jo."*

To escape the pathetic sight, Gabe turned and began to run back, without Pablo. But Pablo sprinted and caught up with him. They ran in unison, even as Gabe picked up speed. He tried to pull away, but should've known he couldn't outrun his friend. As they reached second base, the two slowed to a walk.

"You know that guy?" Pablo asked after catching his breath.

Gabe wiped his sweaty face with the front of his T-shirt. "Yeah," he admitted. "I know him."

"You do?"

"Yeah, he's my dad."

At home, he showered, watched television, and then went to sleep to the squeaking of the swamp cooler. In the middle of the night, he woke to the sound of pie tins rattling. He peered out the window and saw—and heard—movements in the darkness. By then, his mother had turned off the swamp cooler. Crickets chirped in the yard; the neighbor's dog barked twice and then became quiet. On Tulare Street, a bad muffler popped like gunfire.

Someone's in the yard, Gabe thought. He got out of bed and slipped into his jeans. His heart thumped as he tiptoed through the kitchen and opened the back door. Something rubbed against his ankles, spooking him, until he recognized his own cat, Gordo. He petted the cat and slowly descended the steps in his bare feet, amazed that the cement could still be warm from the day.

[Gabe]

A pie tin rattled in the dark.

"Who's there?" Gabe called in a husky voice.

The neighbor's dog offered a single bark in response.

Gabe could just make out the baseball bat propped against the garage. He grabbed the bat and advanced cautiously into the darkened area of the lawn. He waited, listening. The grass was cool and damp compared to the cement, and a chill sent goose bumps up his arms.

Why did dad come back? Gabe asked himself. *Why? Why?*

A strong breeze rattled the pie tins. The neighbor's dog whined, and the crickets, those little insects in armor, once again began to chirp. And then the sound of footsteps in the alley. Gabe hurried to look, his heart charged with terror. Three homies were scaling the neighbor's fence. Had they been in his yard too, disappointed at finding nothing but vine-ripe tomatoes?

Gabe returned to his bedroom. He fell asleep in spite of the heat, and had a nightmare in which he was wading neck-deep in a warm lake. The next morning, he investigated the garden for clues and found two smashed tomatoes and evidence of shoeprints. But whose?

Gabe's dad hadn't always been a deadbeat. One summer, when Gabe was six years old, they had gone to Bass Lake, where mosquitoes, thick as campfire smoke, orbited his head and feasted on his blood. But they'd still had fun fishing, canoeing, and hunting for arrowheads along the riverbank.

Another summer, they had vacationed at Aunt Daisy's home in San José. The grownups got the extra bedroom while the kids—he and his cousins—slept in a tent in the backyard.

"It's like camping," his dad had said, handing them Gatorade bottles refilled with ice-cold water. He gave them each a candy bar, which Gabe and his cousins devoured in seconds. They drifted to sleep with chocolate-covered fingers, then woke screaming before daylight, with ants scurrying down the length of their arms. It was his hero dad who had doused their arms with the garden hose and softly patted away the ants.

Life was good then. His dad worked at Office Depot and had advanced quickly from stock clerk to manager. One December, his dad was named Regional Manager of the Month. For all that hard work, he got to see his photo up on the wall for a month and enjoy a free weekend at a resort in Half Moon Bay.

They'd had fun at the resort. Gabe had collected shells, rocks, wave-polished glass, and seaweed

[Gabe]

that he took home to show friends. But the best experience was the Jacuzzi in their bathroom. How he had giggled and squirmed when his dad picked him up and placed him in the center of the giant tub, jets churning the water.

But even then, Gabe recalled, his dad was beginning to drink.

※

That morning, Gabe's mother announced that she was going to skip work—at least a couple of hours—in order to file a restraining order. Gabe decided to join her.

On the fifth floor of City Hall, there was a long line of strollers and mothers gossiping with other mothers. Some of the babies were like sirens that wouldn't shut up, even when you plugged their mouths with pacifiers.

"*Ay, Dios mío,*" his mother complained under her breath. "It'll be tomorrow by the time I get to the front. Look at all these people."

Gabe was surprised. Were all these women seeking restraining orders against their lousy husbands, exes, or boyfriends? He then recognized Linda Ramirez, a girl from school, who was nervously chewing a fingernail. He forced himself to look away. He didn't want to embarrass her or himself.

"This is ridiculous!" his mom bawled. "I can't wait. I gotta to get to work!"

They rode down the elevator in silence. When the doors opened, Gabe was surprised by the two women waiting for the elevator. Neither seemed happy. One had bruises around her eyes—from lack of sleep, Gabe hoped, and not from being slapped around by a mean husband.

Gabe's mother gave him two dollars for a soda and chips, then drove off in their secondhand Toyota. Gabe started toward the library but became immediately uneasy when he noticed three homies eyeing him like vultures. He recognized one of them—Frankie Torres. He used to hang with Frankie at Romain Playground when they were little. They played a lot of board games back then, and four square and tetherball.

Instinct told Gabe to retreat. He turned on the squeaky heels of his trainers and headed back to City Hall, where he waited inside until Frankie and his crew had passed. Then he headed to the library.

The morning was cloudless, with barely enough breeze to ripple the flags. Gabe stood in the shade of the library entrance, waiting for the doors to be unlocked. There were others waiting too—all homeless people, it seemed. He flapped the front of his T-shirt as he struggled to cool himself off. He considered splurging on a cold soda right then,

[Gabe]

but common sense told him to delay the purchase until it was at least noon.

Then a voice called, "Son! Gabe!"

His dad was walking across the lawn that gleamed wet from the sprinklers. He was holding one hand up to his forehead to shade his eyes from the sun.

"I'm not your son!" Gabe snarled, taking a few steps back.

His dad closed the distance between them, leaving a trail of damp prints on the cement.

"Gabe, please don't be like that."

"Like what?" Gabe asked. His hands were now posted on his hips. "Like I don't see you for like four years and then you show up? Like everything's cool now."

When his dad lowered his face, something small splashed on the pavement. A tear, an errant drop from the sprinkler, or a bead of sweat—Gabe wasn't sure which. The wet speck spread to the size of a dime and began to evaporate in the sun. Gabe regretted his outburst.

"I'm sick," his dad claimed, with a faint, pitiful whine in his voice. "It's my stomach." His dad grimaced when he pressed a hand against his stomach.

Glancing sideways, Gabe saw a security guard flip the library's "Closed" sign to "Open." He heard the jingle of keys and the *clunk-clunk* of the lock.

The homeless crowd, gray as a flock of pigeons, gathered thickly at the door. They were hurrying to get on the Internet or locate the choice seats in the magazine alcove.

"You're lying," Gabe snapped. "You just need a bath. That's your problem."

"See what I have raised," his dad replied, "a mean child."

"You didn't raise anyone!" Gabe was surprised by his anger. "You don't know me. I bet you don't even know my birthday."

"Gabe, please."

"When is it?" Gabe challenged.

"Gabe, come on, give me a chance."

"You don't even know when your own son was born. And you call yourself a father."

"I know, I know," his dad agreed, his hands clasped together, as if in prayer. The long sleeves of his shirt fell back to reveal thin forearms.

They stood in silence, face to face. Against his will, Gabe started to soften. He wondered where his dad bedded down at night. At the Poverello House? The courthouse park? An alley in Chinatown? Or the encampment near the freeway?

"Gabe, I made mistakes." He was in AA, he said—Alcoholics Anonymous. It wasn't a glamorous group. Some of the men were homeless like him. But they were all trying to stay sober and off drugs.

Gabe was uncertain. Was his dad being truthful?

[Gabe]

Was he really sick, deathly sick? The ice around his heart continued to melt, drip by drip. His dad was destitute, with all his worldly possessions in a suitcase that he dragged along like a shadow.

"OK, I get it," he remarked with sorrow in his voice. "You're right."

Gabe's dad turned suddenly and walked away. Gabe thought of calling to him, of calling, "Dad, don't go." But words failed him.

If Gabe's mother hadn't been at work, he would've gone home right away to tell her about the encounter. Instead, he headed to Romain Playground, using a detour that took him through a dilapidated area where sturdy guard dogs barked and snarled at him.

Ever since he was a little kid with scabs on his elbows and knees, Romain Playground had been his second home. There, he climbed the rope of experience. He had his first fight there, received his first kiss (on the cheek), suffered his first injury requiring stitches, and survived his first experience with crime. When he'd been a skinny seven year old, an older kid had pushed him against a backstop, plunged a hand into his pocket, and stole his stash of Tootsie Rolls.

On that morning, he played checkers with a little

girl genius. No one could win against her—not even adults. With a red whip dangling from her mouth, she beat Gabe three times in a row. He moaned when she repeated jokingly, "Oops, I won again."

Gabe suddenly felt out of place. Not until late in the afternoon would kids his own age show up at Romain. With nothing to do, he headed to the rec room, which was a small cinder-block building. Metal mesh on the two windows protected the room against break-ins.

"How's things, homeboy?" Jamal, the rec leader, asked. On his neck hung his playground bling—a whistle that he blew at least once an hour at troublemakers.

Gabe debated whether to burden Jamal with his cargo of hurt. But he figured that Jamal was more than a rec leader; he was like a social worker, too. He readily listened to the worries of the kids who showed up daily. So Gabe just said, "OK, I guess."

"Don't sound OK to me," Jamal said.

At that, Gabe asked, "You got a father?"

The smile on Jamal's face flattened. "Somewhere in this world. My mom and me, we don't talk about the man." He grabbed a pump, which resembled a small rifle. When he began to pump up a four-square ball, the muscles on his forearms rippled. "Why you ask?"

"I saw mine today," Gabe disclosed. "I saw him yesterday, too."

[Gabe]

Jamal punched the ball and sent it rolling to the corner of the rec room, where it settled among three worn basketballs. "Let me guess," Jamal said. "He wasn't around before that, huh?"

Gabe nodded.

"Man, they never around—that's the way it be." Jamal bent down for another ball to inflate. "Half these kids ain't got daddies. You don't, I don't, the little checkers genius girl, she don't." He shook his head and grumbled. "When he split?"

"When I was nine." Gabe replayed the scene of his dad backing out of the driveway, none too slowly. He could still see the right back tire running over the flowerbed beside the driveway, smashing a row of pretty-faced petunias.

"That's 'bout right," Jamal said. "That's when they leave. Mine left, came back, left again." He told Gabe that his father was never coming back.

"Why?" Gabe asked.

"He's in prison, that's why," Jamal answered. "Armed robbery. Doing twenty someplace in Arizona."

Gabe left the playground with a can of root beer, a gift from Jamal, who had the key to the soda machine. As he drank, the foam tickled his nose. The soda was sweet and icy cold—just what he needed.

Gabe paused to watch two boys—ten year olds, he guessed—shaking down a little kid for money.

Gabe almost yelled, "Hey, leave him alone," but he held his tongue. The little kid was pressed against the fence, starched with fear; he was learning a playground lesson: don't carry money in your pocket. Plus, Gabe figured they weren't actually hurting him, and that the kid could always get another quarter, dime, or whatever had been in his pocket. But how else would he learn important things about life?

Gabe drifted to the Fulton Mall, where he killed time at the edge of a dry fountain, brimming with litter. Since it was an outdoor mall, there were few shoppers. Allergic to heat, they wisely took their business to the air-conditioned comfort of indoor malls in north Fresno.

"Hey," a voice called in a near whisper.

Gabe rose cautiously to his feet. How many times had the word *Hey* gotten him in trouble? There had been the *Hey* when an Asian brother tried to sell him a stolen iPod and the *Hey* when a man asked him to hold a ladder steady. How could Gabe have known that the man was stealing copper tubing from the building's roof?

Gabe sized up the *vato loco* swaggering toward him in pants cut off at the knees. The guy was about thirty-years old, a *veterano* of the street. A large *L*

[Gabe]

on a gold chain sparkled on his chest. On his neck, a tattoo of a leaping tiger.

"Hey," Gabe responded, then hitched up his pants. There was no telling if he might be forced to run. Something didn't seem right about a *vato* cradling a puppy in his tattooed arms. Gabe did his best to appear calm, though his thirteen-year-old soul was trembling. What did this guy want?

"You wanna buy a dog?" the *vato* asked. His wrist was tagged with the name Gloria. Gabe supposed that Gloria was his wife or girlfriend, or possibly his ex-girlfriend, or maybe someone else's wife or girlfriend. The dude was wearing cologne but, beneath that nice scent, he stank of bad deeds.

Gabe patted his pockets and said, "I ain't got no money."

"You ain't got money?" howled the *vato*. "But bet you got a phone. That's better than money." His eyes were flecked with anger. "Let me use it—right now, *ese!*" He snapped his fingers for Gabe to hurry up.

Gabe accepted his fate and reached into his back pocket.

"Hold him." The *vato* handed the pup to Gabe.

Gabe took the pup in his arms like it was a baby. He loved dogs, and dogs loved him. When the dog's eyes opened, his tail began to wag.

The *vato* called someone named Bobby, and then made a second call to someone named Marcos. The *vato* scolded Marcos, saying, "If you don't have the money, then you gotta wait. Dude, I'm in business. I'm a businessman these days! Feel me?" The veins on his throat bulged with each hard word and made the tattoo of the leaping tiger bounce.

The *vato* was preparing to hand back the phone when his small eyes brightened. "Hey, little dude, let's trade," he suggested, pointing the phone at the puppy. "My dog for your phone. Pretty fair deal, ain't it?"

Scam artist, Gabe warned himself. He debated whether to grab his phone and run.

"He's a champ," the *vato* claimed. "A rare breed." He looked down at the phone when it began to ring. "Yeah," he answered roughly. His eyes moved in their sockets until his mind pieced together the meaning of the call. He shoved the phone at Gabe. "It's some lady, your mom I think."

Gabe was grateful to take hold of his phone again, and glad his mother was on the other end.

"Hi, Mom," Gabe answered. "What's up?"

His mother told him to take out a round steak from the freezer. The voice she used meant that he had better not forget!

"Good as done," he promised, pocketing his phone. And just like that he could see his time with the *vato* was about to end: the man's eyes had become large with fear.

When Gabe turned around, he understood

[Gabe]

the *vato's* sudden decision to depart. A squad of homies was hustling toward them.

"Take my dog," the *vato* ordered. "I ain't selling him, either. I was just playing with you." He stabbed a finger at Gabe's chest. "I'll be back for him. Don't forget." The *vato* skipped backwards as if he were dancing, then spun around and took off, leaving Gabe with the pup in his arms.

Within seconds, the homies surrounded him.

"You with that fool?" one blasted. He wore his pants low on his hips, and his white T-shirt was so bright that it hurt Gabe's eyes.

"Nah," Gabe replied, hugging the pup to his chest. "The dude just gave me this dog,"

"I know you," another homie said. He searched Gabe's face, as if deciding which feature to punch first: nose, teeth, cheek, or hairless jaw.

Gabe recognized him, too. He was Tony Torres, big brother of Frankie Torres.

"Yeah, you know me," Gabe volunteered. The sweat was steaming up his hair and ready to cascade down into his eyes. "I'm Gabe. I hang at Romain."

The homie who had the word Fresno tattooed on his forehead returned to the question of the *vato loco*. "You know Lupe?"

"Who's Lupe?" Gabe asked, as the significance of the *L* on the imitation gold chain became clear. Gabe had assumed it meant "Loser."

"The fool you be talkin' to, that's who!" the homie barked.

"Nah," Gabe answered. "Like I tole you. He just gave me this dog." He petted the pup's white fur and considered letting him hold the canine as a sign of friendship.

But he didn't get a chance to. Tony grabbed the pup and raised him like a trophy. He inspected the dog, then pronounced, "It's a dude. I was looking for one."

The homies left with the pup, who was still wagging his tail. There was joy in the dog no matter whose arms held hm.

Shaken, Gabe sat down on the edge of the fountain. Without water, it had become a wastebasket for shoppers who strolled past, sipping sodas and crunching churros. When he'd been little, he had tossed coins into the fountain and made a wish each time. If he'd had any change, even a penny, he would've tossed it in and wished for a quick escape. Tony was cruel.

The Poverello House was located in a part of Fresno once lined with factories where workers packed fruit, mainly plums and peaches. Now the area was swarming with transients. Gabe stood a short distance away from two men shouting and

[Gabe]

pushing each other. Were these two men, their hair stringy as dirty mops, arguing over the large woman hovering over a shopping cart? Gabe hoped not.

"Hey!"

Gabe spun around to find a shirtless brother, with a sombrero on his head, approaching. With each long step, his stomach rippled with muscles. Gabe wondered if he was starving, or if he still retained the muscle tone of his high school years. He had the body of a hurdler.

"You Mexican, ain't you?" the brother asked.

"Yeah," Gabe answered.

He smiled, revealing a space where his front teeth should be. He ran a hand along the brim of his sombrero. "I bet you like this sporty attire."

Gabe could tell it was a decorative sombrero from the wall of a Mexican restaurant.

"It's all right." Gabe pushed his hands into his back pockets. Another scam was in progress.

"What you mean—'all right'?" The brother removed the sombrero from his head, displaying a shiny bald head, and claimed loudly, "This here is an antique. It's like a piece of cultural history."

Gabe suspected the tag inside the sombrero that read, "Hecho in China."

"I got it off this fellow who said it belonged to his grandfather—fought in one of your wars down where they speak Spanish so fast you don't know what they be saying." He spun the sombrero on a frighteningly long fingernail. "I ain't asking much, just enough to put a taco and chips in my belly."

When Gabe said that he didn't have any money, the brother fumed, "How come I only meet poor folks?" He shook his head and looked into the distance. Then, without a goodbye, he hustled away with the sombrero back on his head.

Gabe scanned the dozens of men—and women—ghosting in front of the Poverello House. Most were pushing shopping carts or hauling plastic bags of aluminum cans and plastic bottles over their shoulders. There was no rest for the weary, even on this hot day.

No mistake about it. These were hard times in Fresno.

※

Gabe embarked on the two-mile trek back to his neighborhood, down one residential street after another. He noticed some houses were tidy and others so littered with junk on the lawn that they looked like crummy yard sales. Along the way, he had a nice bit of luck. On the sidewalk lay a dollar bill. Without a thought, he snatched up that crisp, sun-dried greenback.

It was midday. After a mile, with sweat pouring out of him, he stopped at a house where the sprinklers were misting the overwatered lawn. One

[Gabe]

of the sprinkler heads was broken and was more like a bubbler. He got down and drank from it. At that moment, water never tasted so good.

But Gabe desired something sweeter than water. Most sodas at 7-Eleven cost a dollar and some change, but Gabe knew a liquor store where sixteen-ounce sodas cost only eighty-nine cents. As he approached the liquor store, he was surprised by the horde of people out front. He started to hurry when he saw two television crews. A robbery? Blood spilled from a parking-lot fight? Or maybe both!

Gabe found out that the store had sold a winning Lotto ticket. At first, he heard someone say a million dollars, but as he listened to the gossip, in English and Spanish, he learned that the prize was actually ten thousand dollars.

The amount was disappointing. Gabe could feel the excitement drain out of him, like a punctured swim toy slowly losing air. With a million dollars, he could set his mom up in a new house in a nice area. With ten thousand dollars, he might be able to buy a secondhand car when he got his driver's license.

But still!

The winners were the Ramirez family—the family of Linda Ramirez, whom he'd seen at City Hall! Just that morning she had been nervously chewing her fingernail in the hallway as her mom waited in line to get a restraining order. Now his classmate was smiling for the camera, her teeth white as Chiclets. Her mother had a chubby arm around Linda and her little brother.

Gabe entered the liquor store. There was no one behind the cash register. Except for the fan at the counter, fluttering the pages of an open magazine, the place was quiet. Gabe headed to the refrigerated case, grabbed a soda from the back, where they were the coldest, and left his found dollar bill on the counter.

At home, Gabe listened to the phone message on their ancient answering machine—Coach Rodriguez saying practice was at 6:00p.m. He ate two bologna sandwiches with a pile of chili-flavored Fritos and was watching television when he remembered the round steak in the freezer. He pulled it out, set it on the kitchen counter to defrost, and went into the backyard to water the flowerbed and tomato plants.

Gordo was stretched out under the picnic table.

"Man, you must be hot," Gabe remarked.

The cat raised its head, blinked.

Poor cat, Gabe thought, dressed in fur on a day like this. He went back inside for a handful of ice cubes. He returned outside and set them floating

[Gabe]

like glaciers in the cat bowl. He had picked up Gordo and was bringing him to his bowl when a voice called out, "Gabe, these are pretty tasty."

Through the haze of afternoon heat, his dad loomed over the vegetable garden, gripping a red tomato the size of a cue ball. Gabe poured Gordo gently from his arms.

"I just want to see you," his dad explained. He bit into the tomato, juice squirting onto his shirt.

Gabe remained silent. His dad, he could see, was thinner than he imagined, a scarecrow in the garden.

"I looked for you," Gabe admitted. He lifted an arm and pointed south towards the Poverello House.

"Is that right," his dad remarked. He moved a few steps toward Gabe. "And where was that?"

"Downtown," Gabe answered. He noticed the plastic medical band on his dad's wrist. "Are you *really* sick or just pretending?"

"Had some blood work done, that's all," his dad answered. He stepped slowly into the shade and lowered his gaze at Gordo drinking from his water bowl. "Is that Sammy?"

"Nah, Sammy's in cat heaven." Sammy had been their trickster cat, who lived at least thirteen adventurous lives. The last one was used up when he tried to cross the street. "This is Gordo. He's a pound cat."

His dad smiled and whispered, "Gordo." He

tossed the half-eaten tomato away and wiped his fingers on his pants.

"I could fix you a sandwich," Gabe said. He was worried that his dad wasn't eating.

"Nah, Gabe," he replied and hesitatingly added, "But thanks." He eased himself down into a plastic chair and sighed. "I could use a cold drink, though."

Without hesitation, Gabe climbed the back steps into the kitchen, poured a glass of water with ice, and returned hurriedly to the yard.

"Thanks, son," his dad said. He took a long drink and pressed the glass against his forehead. When he pulled it away, rivulets of dirt began to form on his brow. He touched the muddy moisture, studied it for a moment, and then wiped it on his pants.

"Dad," Gabe began. "I'm sorry."

"You're sorry," his dad said. "That's what I'm supposed to say." He emptied the glass in a long swallow, rattled the ice cubes, and confessed, "I'm an alcoholic, Gabe, pure and simple. Been like this for years." He flung the ice cubes from his glass so that they tumbled like dice across the patio. "How long do you think they'll last?"

Gabe looked briefly at the ice cubes but didn't answer. He could smell the stink of street living. He felt that his dad would feel better if he only had a shower.

His dad glanced at the cat, let a smile rise on his stubbly face and asked, "What's its name again?"

[Gabe]

"Gordo," Gabe answered.

His dad chuckled then began to cough into both hands. He cleared his throat and reached for a pack of cigarettes in his shirt pocket.

"Don't smoke, Dad."

His dad frowned and returned his cigarettes to his shirt pocket. "Yeah, OK." He bent down and tickled the scruff of Gordo's neck.

"I'll be back," Gabe said. He rushed up the back steps into the house. He went into his bedroom and pawed through the drawers for clothes. From the bathroom medicine cabinet, he retrieved a toothbrush, a partially used tube of toothpaste, a bar of soap, and a tiny bottle of hotel shampoo. If his dad was willing, Gabe would bathe him on the lawn. That would help bring him back to clean living.

"Oh, Dad," he muttered, his lower lip trembling. "I won't let you die."

Gabe wiped a long tear from his right eye. He searched frantically for a razor, but when he couldn't find one he hurried outside to the patio.

"Dad?" he called. "Dad!" His father was nowhere in sight.

A pie tin banged among the tomato plants. The neighbor's dog barked. Down the street a gardener was starting up a leaf blower. Gabe returned to the shade of the patio awning. The ice cubes that his father had tossed were nearly puddles now, disappearing as he watched.

At five in the afternoon, his mother came home, her Walmart nametag sagging on the front of her blouse.

"We were robbed today," she said, slipping out of her shoes. "Gabe, get me a glass of water, with ice." She strode to the hallway and let the ceiling vent of their cooler blow on her. "Ah, that feels good."

"Robbed?" Gabe, sitting in front of the television, rose to his feet. When he punched the remote, the image of a baseball player collapsed and disappeared. He started toward the kitchen.

"These three stupid kids!" she scolded, as if it was partly his fault.

Frankie and his crew, Gabe imagined. Or fools like them.

Gabe's mom moved from the hallway to the recliner. She took her cold drink from Gabe. "Then the stupidest one comes up to Marta," she continued. "The kid says to Marta, '*Vieja*, give me the money!'" His mom plopped down, drained the glass, and continued. "Marta's got her register closed. She can't open it unless you buy something. And how rude to call her an old lady! She's only a year older than me."

She told Gabe how the boy ran out, dropping a load of watches, candy, batteries, shampoo, and

[Gabe]

sponges in the parking lot. He had stuffed everything in his baggy pants, but the pants couldn't stay up on his skinny hips.

"Sponges?" Gabe asked. "The dude stole sponges?"

"Yeah, I said he was the stupidest. He could have taken his *nalgas* down to the Dollar Store and robbed them for way cheaper."

Gabe remained quiet for a few minutes before he said, "Dad was here."

She studied him through tired eyes.

"He doesn't look right. Mom, he's sick."

"You don't have to tell me your father's sick. I lived with him." She tapped a finger against her temple. "He's sick up here."

She turned her head toward the television, which was turned off. Her reflection on the darkened screen resembled one of the women on her favorite soap opera.

"He wants to come home," Gabe said.

"He doesn't have a home," she answered quickly. She raised her glass and rolled a chunk of ice into her mouth.

"Mom, I know—"

"You don't know!" she snapped. One hand gripped the doily on the recliner's arm, like a claw. She looked down and pouted. "I broke a nail." Then she apologized: "Sorry, Gabe. He just makes me so mad."

The debate was over.

Gabe found sanctuary in his bedroom, where he lay on his bed, arms behind his head. His dad, he reflected, had been a lousy husband and not much of a father. He had loathed this absent man for years. Whenever he had come across a photograph of him, Gabe had been tempted to crumple it in his fist. But now his father was a man hauling a dirty suitcase. Now he was sick.

He heard his mother in the kitchen, frying the round steak. When he ventured in, she was shaking the handle of a large skillet, angrily shoving it back and forth. Her eyes were wet. Had she been crying—or were the tears from dicing the onion?

"Set the table," she ordered.

"I have a game tonight," he began to explain. "It's too hot to eat."

"You're going to eat with me." She began to grate cheese on the *frijoles* simmering on the back burner.

Gabe pictured Coach Rodriguez, scanning the dugout and counting his players. "Thompson, Sanchez, Padilla, Romero. . . Hey, where's Mendoza?" Coach was unforgiving when players were late. He would point him to the bench and keep him there all seven innings.

Still, he set the table as his mother had asked. He poured a glass of iced tea for her, and a glass of strawberry-flavored Kool-Aid for himself.

[Gabe]

They ate in silence until his mother asked, "How did he look?"

"Sick."

"What does 'sick' mean? Like he's skinny?" She prodded a cherry tomato with a fork. "He could be lying, you know."

Gabe had considered this possibility. His dad had spun many tales of deceit. When his father had bought him his first bicycle, for example, he'd told Gabe that it was new. Gabe was six at the time, but he knew new from old, truth from a lie. The bicycle—with its training wheels and bright plastic ribbons dangling from the handle grips—had belonged to some other child first. There were tiny pebbles embedded in the tread of the tires, and the reflector in the back was cracked.

"Yeah, Mom, he's skinny. And he has a thing on his wrist."

"What do you mean, 'thing'?" Gabe's mother lanced the cherry tomato and lifted the fork to her mouth.

"Like a bracelet. Like from when you're in the hospital."

His mother chewed with her head down, pushing the rice and *frijoles* around her plate. Gabe could tell that she wasn't relishing her dinner.

"Mom, he says he's sorry," Gabe said.

"And I should care?" Her eyes glared at him until he looked down at his plate. She spooned salsa onto the *frijoles* and tore a piece of tortilla. "You think he's nice because he says he's sorry? Big deal!" She brought the tortilla laden with *frijoles* to her mouth.

"I'm just saying, you know, he's better." Gabe had lost his appetite. He bullied his *frijoles* around the plate. Why does she take it out on me?

"I don't care. I don't want him to come around!"

Mother and son, napkins in their fists, ate in silence.

When Gabe showed up at the game, their team was down 4–5 in the third inning. Coach Rodriguez posted his hands on his hips and spat, "Get in the dugout, Mendoza." He slapped a clipboard against his thigh, raising dust from his pants.

Gabe obeyed without a word. He was clutching two shopping bags filled with supplies for his dad. He had intended—and still intended—to confide in Coach Rodriguez. But for now he sat at the far end of the dugout, his mitt at his side. Neither of the teams was playing well. Even the weakest hits skipped through holes in the infield.

By the fifth inning, the score was 9–7, Kerman in the lead. Most of the Kerman players had reached base by walks, when the Fresno pitcher couldn't find the strike zone. Coach Rodriguez stood with his arms folded across his muscle-plated chest. He

[Gabe]

was not in the least happy when in the sixth inning an unfamiliar figure appeared in deep center field. All of the players turned their eyes on him, this person.

"It's Dad," Gabe muttered to himself. When the game was halted, he scrambled out of the dugout.

The umpire, strolling out past second base, called, "Buddy! You! Off the field!" He hooked a thumb, as if giving the "out" sign. "You're holding up the game!"

Gabe hustled along the first base line and into right field. "Dad," he yelled, "you're in the middle of the game."

"It's not practice?" his dad asked innocently.

"No, it's for real."

His dad seemed genuinely baffled. A game, a real game?

Gabe escorted his dad off the field, but not without noticing three homies grouped near the kiddie pool. They were staring at Gabe.

"I'll be right back," Gabe told his father. "Don't leave." He hustled to the dugout to retrieve the bags of clothes and personal items. Coach Rodriguez eyed him not so much with anger but with suspicion, as if asking, "Who's the man?"

The players in the dugout watched Gabe too, until they heard the *thwock* of a batter being hit by a pitch. The ball had clocked him in his thigh.

Gabe returned to find his dad hoisting a cigarette

to his lips. He was striking a match when Gabe said, "You can't smoke here." He set the bags on the bench.

His dad lifted his heavy brows, appraised his son, and then tucked the cigarette behind his ear. When the crowd shouted, he looked back at the field. Two players were chugging around the bases. "Looks like someone scored."

They sat together on the bench, the bags between them.

"Dad, just tell me. Are you really sick?"

"My stomach hurts," he answered. "I can't keep food down."

Gabe looked at the plastic hospital bracelet. Was his father being truthful?

"I brought you some clean clothes," Gabe said, peeking into one of the bags. "And stuff you can use."

His dad seemed not to care—no smile, no nothing. His attention returned to the cigarette that he pulled from behind his ear. It had to be a temptation, Gabe thought, because his lips were slightly parted and trembling.

"I don't belong here. I got to go." His dad rose and touched the brim of Gabe's baseball cap. "I'll see you when I'm better."

"Better?"

"When I'm cleaned up," he clarified. Then he started to walk away, the cigarette already in his mouth.

[Gabe]

"Dad, your stuff."

His dad paused, smiled, and remarked weakly, "Yeah, my stuff." He picked up the bags without asking what they contained. "Thanks, Gabe."

His dad ambled away, skirting the outfield, where the center fielder stood with a large mitt hanging at his side. Gabe almost ran after him, but he sensed that his dad was embarrassed about something. His hurt was not his weary bones, or his abused liver or damaged kidneys. The hurt was closer to his heart.

After the game ended, Gabe walked into the parking lot, intending to cross the street for a bag of sunflower seeds and a soda. He didn't get far. The vultures who'd been lurking by the kiddie pool approached him. The big vulture was Frankie Torres. He was taller than Gabe now, certainly meaner, and maybe stronger inside his baggy clothes. Or was it just the way he was walking, with a swagger, his hands out like a gunslinger?

"Hey, ugly!" Frankie barked.

Gabe didn't stop and turn around.

"I said, 'Hey, ugly'!" Frankie barked again.

Gabe could hear the scramble of running feet and noticed shadows swinging to his left. He turned to face Frankie. The shell of a pumpkin seed hung from Frankie's lower lip. When he licked his lip, the shell tumbled to the asphalt.

"This is Holmes," Frankie roared, "not Romain—fool, you at the wrong playground!"

Gabe closed his hands into fists. He was sandwiched between the homies, like a little brown piece of bologna. Frankie had gotten bigger and wicked—and even more stupid. He had a homemade tattoo etched near his thumb, a little red cross. He also had bling tucked into his white T-shirt.

"Get outta here!" Frankie pushed a finger into Gabe's chest.

"Don't touch me!" Gabe warned as he inflated his chest. He couldn't back down to Frankie. "I'm on the team that plays here."

"You mean the team that lost?"

Gabe didn't answer back. He could see the Kerman team milling near a white vans, the engine and air conditioner running. The Kerman coach was handing out bottles of water. Gabe could have used a cold one right then. His mouth was dry with fear.

"You play like a girl," Frankie slurred.

"Nah, the other team played better than us."

Frankie's homies were shorter than Frankie. They were fifth graders, maybe sixth graders, learning their trade on the street.

"Come on, Frankie, I like known you for years," Gabe pleaded. "Why you treating me this way? I didn't do nothing to you."

[Gabe]

Frankie sneered and pushed his face so close to Gabe's that they were almost kissing. His breath smelled of Cheetos.

Gabe had had enough. He stepped back, sucked in a lungful of air, and yelled, "Why you sound so stupid, Frankie?"

"WHAT!" Frankie bellowed, his eyes wide with anger.

"What? Here's what!"

Gabe palm-slapped Frankie on the side of the head then followed with a left-right combination to his stomach. He pushed away and bobbed with his fists up. "Do something!" Gabe snarled. "Try to hit me! I'll make you bleed!"

While Frankie was bent over, catching his breath, the littlest homie threw a roundhouse punch that glanced off Gabe's shoulder. Gabe stepped back and threw a clean shot into the boy's nose. Blood blossomed like a red carnation. The little homie bent over, holding his nose with both hands.

Then it was on, a scrum under the amber lights of the parking lot, fists like windmills. Gabe took a barrage of hits as Frankie and the third homie began to bang. There were moans, and the sound of knuckles against faces, elbows raking jaws, and off-balance kicks that grazed forearms and thighs. Gabe was rocked twice, but he kept his hands up, bouncing on his tiptoes, like a real fighter. He was getting shots in and taking a few, too. He wiped his knuckles against his pants—one of the homies had greasy hair.

Coach Rodriguez, lugging a duffel bag, appeared at the gate. He called, "Hey! Hey!"

Gabe rocked the littlest homie a second time, then stepped away. He touched his own mouth and discovered blood on his fingertips. His right eye was tearing up.

"I'll get you later!" Frankie cried. "You're like dead."

Gabe didn't answer. He was bent over, out of breath, a string of blood dangling like dental floss from his mouth.

As Coach Rodriguez approached in long, purposeful strides, Frankie skipped backward, aware that the fight was over. He sneered and raised a middle finger first at Gabe, then the coach. He fled with the two homies flanking him.

Coach placed a large comforting hand on Gabe's shoulder, then began to examine his face. There was some swelling around Gabe's mouth, a puffy eye, and an ear that pulsed red. He gripped Gabe's chin and turned it left, then right. "You'll be OK," he said. He knelt on one knee and reached into his duffle bag for the first-aid kit. He opened it up. He began to dab Gabe's wounds with rubbing alcohol.

Gabe flinched from the rough swabbing of a Q-tip. There was nothing soft about Coach. His hands were huge.

[Gabe]

"Was that Frankie?" Coach asked. He began to unwrap a square-shaped Band-Aid.

"I don't know," Gabe lied. He pictured Frankie on a prison cot—that's where he was headed for a long time.

Coach Rodriguez scanned the part of the playground where Frankie and his wannabe homies had vanished. He asked, "And who was that man?"

"What man?"

"The man in the outfield, the one you were talking to." He clapped shut the first-aid kit.

Gabe hesitated before answering, "My father." He touched his mouth, which felt hot and swollen.

As Pablo joined them, Gabe spat blood and spat out the story of his messed-up family life and how his father had abandoned him—what, four years ago? Gabe counted the years on his fingers. "Nah, more like five years ago."

Coach Rodriguez bit his lower lip. "I'm sorry to hear all this," he said. His eyes seemed to darken. "I had a father like that, too."

"But mine is like homeless."

Coach Rodriguez grumbled at this personal information. He handed Gabe and Pablo each a bottle of cold water. "You need a ride home?"

"Nah, I got my bicycle behind the dugout."

But he was wrong. When Gabe and Pablo returned to the dugout, they discovered both their bikes were gone.

Gabe removed the Band-Aid from his face before opening the front door. He didn't want to worry his mother, who, he discovered, was on the couch. She had the remote in her hand and was watching a repeat of *Project Runway*. When he broke the news about his bike, she furrowed her brow and asked, "What happened to your lip? Were you in a fight?"

Gabe told her that a grounder had kicked up and smacked him in the face.

She didn't believe him for one second. His mom was no fool. She frowned and said, "Gabe, stay out of trouble—please."

After taking a shower, Gabe spooned out the center of a cold watermelon. On the couch, he watched a bout of mixed martial arts on television, then reluctantly visited his bedroom. It was still an oven. Although the swamp cooler was churning at full speed, the house's stucco held in the day's heat. He raised a window: no breeze.

Gabe slept uneasily. At three in the morning, the pie tins in the garden began to bang. He peered out his window, waiting and listening. Minutes later, he heard grass crunching under footsteps and swore that he could make out a dark running shadow.

Who? Who was it?

After a while, he fell back to sleep.

[Gabe]

When he woke, his mom had already gone to work. Gabe fixed himself a plate of *huevos con weenies*, plus two tortillas and a glass of milk. To finish off his breakfast, he ate three Oreo cookies. He was washing these down with a second glass of milk when Pablo called on the landline phone.

Early that morning, Pablo had returned to the playground, where he found their bikes stripped—the handlebars, pedals, and seats were gone. Even worse, the spokes were kicked in. Whoever stole the bikes had punished them for fun.

"Come and see for yourself," Pablo said.

He walked a mile to Pablo's house, not in the least concerned about the vato locos who sat on high porches, shirtless and tattooed, watching, always watching. Their running days were over. They were fathers and husbands (or ex-husbands) now with front-row seats to la vida loca, the crazy times in the neighborhood. This was their entertainment—sodas, beer, sunflower seeds and a view of every car, truck, baby stroller, bike, skateboard, scooter and wheelchair that rolled up the street.

When Gabe gazed at the remains of their bikes behind Pablo's garage, his hands closed into fists. "You think Frankie did it?"

"Nah, the *tonto* didn't have time. He was too busy playing with his wannabes." Pablo peered at Gabe's face and asked: "Does it hurt?"

Gabe touched his tender lip, which was much

less puffy. "Nah, not really." Squatting, he plucked music from a bent spoke.

"We'll never know who messed up our bikes," Pablo said calmly. "But I'm gonna get some new wheels."

Gabe knew where they were headed. They would visit Manny Treviño, a *pinto* who sold bikes and bike parts from his garage. You could put in an order for anything, including car parts, and Manny would do his best to get it for you. The prices were good, and the merchandise first-rate, though usually stolen.

Manny was a heavyset man who wore oil-stained jeans obscenely low on his wide hips. His white T-shirt was anything but white, mostly grease stained. He was a veteran of the streets of southeast Fresno. He had done six months here, six months there. His last stop for time-out was Happy Valley Prison near Coalinga, where he plucked chickens at the prison meat-processing factory. In exchange, he only had to serve four months of a nine-month sentence, and he got the chance to learn about poultry. He learned so much that he vowed never to eat chicken again.

Manny's wife answered the door in a bathrobe, pink slippers, and a pile of curlers on her head—queen of her own household. She told Gabe and Pablo that Manny wasn't home, and he was not about to come home anytime soon. He had been busted

[Gabe]

trying to sell a stolen laptop to an undercover cop. He was back at Happy Valley, getting reacquainted with poultry.

"Did he care about me?" she roared, scorching their ears. "No, I tole the fool to stick to bicycles and skateboards, but what does he do? Gets a big head! Thinks there's more money in computers and phones!"

The two boys hurried away, wondering what to do next. They didn't have to wonder long because Frankie Torres was sliding up the street, with a larger posse than usual—the two little homies-in-training, plus three new boys who were as large as refrigerators. They were wearing white T-shirts that hung to their knees.

"Dang!" Pablo remarked. "Let's get outta here!"

Gabe was glad that he had double-knotted his shoelaces. The two bolted up the street, past dogs barking behind chain-link fences and the old-school *vato locos* enjoying the action from high porches.

Gabe figured that he and Pablo had to live long enough to at least start seventh grade.

The two boys found safe haven at Romain Playground. Jamal, the rec leader, was outside playing four square with three barefoot little kids. If Frankie showed up and started stuff, Jamal would grab him by the back of the neck, shove him out the gate, and yell, "I don't wanna see your ugly face for a week! Get out, fool!"

They played checkers with the genius girl and lost four times, even when they helped the other with strategies. The boys left the playground, skirted the block of Section 8 housing and crossed Belmont Avenue, stopping at a liquor store for sodas, which they drank in hurried gulps. Hungry for something solid, they tripped back into the store and bought powdery donuts, then began meandering toward Gabe's house.

On Angus Street, someone shouted from a porch, "Hey, little dude, what happened to my dog?"

Gabe stopped in his tracks. When he turned, he was surprised to see Lupe, the *vato loco* from the Fulton Mall. Shirtless, Lupe was tagged with tattoos from his chest to his belly button. His hair had been cropped so close that his skull looked blue.

"What you do with my dog?" Lupe asked roughly. He came down the wooden steps, hitching up his pants.

Gabe could see that Lupe was built, scarred from fights, and possibly dangerous. But he was old-school now, and wiser, with a devilish beard on his chin. He was a father, too. In the yard, there was a toppled-over stroller, a tricycle, and a blow-up swimming pool, with flakes of grass floating on the surface of the water.

[Gabe]

"They took him after you ran away," Gabe began to explain.

Lupe sneered. "You think I ran because of *them*? Those freaks!" He pointed at the tattooed his chest. "I don't run from nobody, *ese*."

"You must be fast," Gabe remarked.

"What you mean, homeboy—'You must be fast'?" Lupe stepped toward Gabe, who could smell hair gel and cigarettes. "You think I'm scared of those lowlifes? I banged a lot of heads in my time. Feel what I'm saying? Even got stabbed twice—and I'm still here!" Lupe stared hotly at Gabe.

"I didn't mean it like that, Lupe."

Still, Gabe replayed the scene in the Fulton Mall. Yes, Lupe had fled when Tony Torres and his crew spotted him.

"I didn't mean run, you know. I meant you had to, like, leave," Gabe babbled. His scalp was releasing sweat and fear.

Lupe wagged his head at Gabe. "You a bad liar, little dude." He hooked his thumb at Pablo and asked, "Who's your *carnal*?"

Pablo, who had been standing behind Gabe, edged a few steps toward Lupe. He shoved his hands into his back pockets.

"Pablo. We play softball together."

Lupe lifted his chin in greeting, and Pablo returned the gesture. Lupe then hitched up his pants and said, "You know where I been?"

Gabe shook his head.

"Been to your place." Lupe smiled, revealing a single gold tooth. He told Gabe that he had gone to his house to fetch the puppy. "Whatta you do, keep him inside where it's cool?" He looked skyward and winced. "Been hecka hot this week."

Gabe could see that Lupe was the mystery man in the yard at night. And he hadn't come for ripe tomatoes but for the puppy. Was he raising him for dogfights?

"Nah, Lupe, those guys took it."

"You mean Tony?" The grin on his wide face suddenly vanished.

"Yeah, Tony," Gabe answered.

"*Mala suerte*," Lupe muttered and stared at the ground for a few seconds. He then invited Gabe and Pablo into his backyard. He pulled open a squeaky wrought-iron gate and maneuvered past two dusty cars up on cement blocks.

"Don't be scared," Lupe told Gabe. "I ain't gonna hurt you. Wanna show why I want my pup back."

The yard was home to six pit bulls, two of them licking their moist chops. The other four narrowed their eyes at Pablo, who hoisted a frightened smile, clicked his fingers as a sign of friendship, and sang, "Be cool, dogs."

When one of the pit bulls began to sniff Gabe's shoes, Lupe remarked, "What did you do—step in dog poop? He smells you, *ese*."

[Gabe]

"Nah, he's smelling my cat," Gabe explained.

"Your cat!" Lupe exploded. "Cats ain't nowhere. They ain't loyal. You don't feed 'em for one lousy day, and they gone." Lupe's face looked as stern and soulless as a snake's. Then he smiled and pounded Gabe's back in a friendly way. "It's OK if you like cats. But dogs is where it is. Know what I mean?"

"Yeah, I know what you mean," agreed Gabe. He did his best to smile.

Lupe began to describe his business plan for breeding guard dogs. "And you probably thought I was raising them to fight. That's messed up. Dogfights is like evil." He grabbed the snout of one dog and shook it like a hand. Then he scratched goo from the corners of the dog's eyes and wiped his fingers on his pants. "These guys love me. They would die for me. I would die for them."

"Yeah, they seem loyal," Pablo responded weakly.

Lupe ruffled the scruff of the sturdiest dog. "This dog is named Pretty."

To Gabe the dog was ugly.

"This one here is Picas, and this one is Tiger." Tiger bared his teeth and his tail became stiff as a tree branch. He pointed and said, "And those rascals don't got names yet. Just got 'em yesterday."

Lupe suddenly became sullen. He cracked his knuckles and snarled under his breath, "So Tony took my pup?"

Gabe shrugged his shoulders.

"What's that mean—yes or no?"

"Yes," Gabe answered.

At that, Lupe stepped within inches of Gabe and tapped his chest with a finger. "You know what?"

Gabe remained still. His upper lip had grown a mustache of sweat.

"I want you to go get the dog from Tony."

"Me!" Gabe asked, pointing at himself. "You want *me* to get the dog?"

"Yeah, you. Where you live, it's dangerous. You need a guard dog. You need protection. Feel me?"

Gabe swallowed twice and issued a meager, "Yeah, I know what you mean." He imagined a dozen Frankies running after him. Is that what Lupe meant by dangerous?

"He's yours. Raise him good. And don't buy him cheap dog food—buy him the best they got at Costco's. *Tu sabes*?"

Gabe was glad that Lupe wasn't into dogfighting. He wiggled the fingers of his right hand and let Pretty snort and lick them. He didn't feel afraid of the pit bull anymore. After all, what did he have to fear? The dog was whipping his tail in friendship.

※

Gabe went alone. He hopped the fence, crouched behind a dumpster brimming with foul-smelling

[Gabe]

garbage, and glanced at the puppy sleeping by the back porch. He had a rope tied around his neck. His water bowl was tipped over, and an empty can of dog food lay nearby. Flies buzzed around the puppy's head like a halo.

I'm gonna save him, Gabe promised. He pictured himself running with the pup in his arms and Tony and Frankie chasing after them.

Gabe could hear music inside the house, a loud television, and the party sounds of laughter and cuss words. He heard the refrigerator door slam, then a girl scream, "YOU STOP THAT, YOU STUPID!"

You're all stupid, Gabe thought.

When the back door swung open, Frankie appeared with a Popsicle stick in his mouth. He came barefoot down the steps, flicked the Popsicle stick at the puppy, and disappeared into the garage next to the house. Gabe could hear rummaging sounds. Minutes later, Frankie tottered out with a case of sodas. Before returning inside, he tickled the puppy's chin with a toe. He laughed when the puppy sniffed and licked the toe. Then he roughly poked his foot into the puppy's side. The little dog yelped.

I'm gonna get him, Gabe swore. He would find Frankie all alone and poke a foot into his side. Gabe envisioned how the poke might become a kick, and the kick might become a stomp. We'll see if he laughs then, Gabe thought angrily.

But that was sometime for the future. For now, Gabe had to retrieve the puppy. The stench from the overfilled dumpster was making him dizzy, and he could hear stirring sounds coming from within. Were rats in there, feasting on spoiled grub?

When Gabe rushed forward, the puppy rose to his big floppy feet and wagged his tail. He pulled on the rope and marched in place. There was happiness in his small body.

"Come on," he muttered anxiously. The knot was tight, his fingers clumsy. He wished he had a knife to cut through the rope.

Then Gabe made out the sounds of footsteps in the kitchen. Was Frankie coming back outside—or maybe his older brother, Tony? Gabe quickly tiptoed inside the garage and retreated toward the far wall, careful to not kick anything over. His hands were trembling. In the oven-like heat of the garage, sweat moistened his armpits.

"Dang," Gabe muttered as he eyes became accustomed to the dark.

In the garage were stacks and stacks of sodas, bottled water, canned foods, cereals, cases of Top Ramen and Pampers, and bags of quality dog food, along with fifty-pound bags of rice and pinto beans. Were they expecting a famine? The garage resembled a small version of a Costco warehouse. Gabe figured the stuff was stolen. Maybe the Torres family needed a dog to guard their loot. And there

[Gabe]

was no telling what they had inside the house: iPods still in their packaging, boxes of new basketball shoes, soccer balls, stolen laptops stacked to the ceiling? Knockoff Hollister T-shirts?

Anything was possible.

Just then Frankie came into the garage. He stepped over a case of SpaghettiOs and another of Campbell's soup, then, ostrich-like, bent over to pick up a box of Rice-A-Roni. He tossed the box into the air and caught it, and started back to the house.

The heat within the garage was smothering Gabe. He reached down and quietly tore open a case of bottled water. He took a bottle and drank its warm contents, then poured some of the water on the back of his neck and wiped his face with the front of his T-shirt. He tiptoed back to the door and peered out onto the patio, grateful for fresh air.

The puppy was gnawing at his rope. He was no dummy, Gabe thought. Even he had the instinct to escape. The pup, suddenly aware of Gabe in the doorway, stood up, his tail wagging in happiness.

Gabe made his move. He struggled to get the puppy's head out of the noose, but paused momentarily when the puppy whined and barked. Would the sound bring Frankie to the back door? He waited and listened. When he didn't hear footsteps, he continued working at the noose until the puppy's head finally slipped through.

Gabe scampered away with the puppy in his arms.

※

Home was six blocks away, under the sun's fierce glare, and the journey was more difficult than Gabe had imagined. The puppy kept wriggling in his arms to get down. When Gabe lowered him to the sidewalk, the puppy stopped and sniffed every leaf, candy wrapper, smashed soda can, and crooked line of ants hauling goodies to their hole. Everything was exciting, everything was new.

"Come on, let's go," Gabe begged as the dog began to nibble on grass.

Suddenly, Gabe had a different reason to get going. Two shirtless older teenagers were staring at him from the porch of a nearby house. They were like vampires, unwilling to step out into the daylight. They would hang on the porch until the net of dusk began to shroud the neighborhood. Only then would they saunter down the wooden stairs. Then, with their vampire eyes, they would scan the world for something to steal with their hands or someone to hurt with their fists. They would draw blood from a passerby and drink it down.

"Get over here!" one of the vampires yelled. He had been killing time in a white plastic chair, and now he stood up. His pants hung low on his waist,

[Gabe]

revealing striped boxers. The muscles on his chest shone like trophies. His belly button, like the eye of a Cyclops, seemed to glare at Gabe, too.

Gabe pretended not to hear.

"Fool, I said, get over here!" The vampire snapped his fingers as if Gabe were a dog. His friend chuckled, then stood up, revealing a wobbly gut. He threw a tomato at Gabe, and tomato rolled into the street, splitting apart.

Gabe swung the puppy into his arms and began to walk away, then trot. The puppy's ears flopped with each stride. But he hadn't gone far when on their bikes the wheeling shadows of the two vampires overtook him. One of them slapped Gabe on the back of his head as he rode by.

"What you doin' on *our* street?" he snarled, then circled back.

Gabe stopped, head down, and peered into the innocent eyes of his puppy. Gabe realized that he was dead meat.

Both gangsters came to a skidding stop in front of him.

"Don't you go ears? *Mi carnal* asked you a question!" the slim vampire roared. He had grilles in his red mouth—blood or the juice from a red-colored Jolly Rancher?

"I didn't hear you," Gabe lied.

The two vampires looked at each other and smirked.

"You smell," the chubby vampire growled. "Say, 'I smell like a *pedo*.'" He nudged the front tire of his bike against Gabe's shin. Then he spat at Gabe's shoes and missed.

Gabe clamped his mouth shut. He stepped back when the chubby vampire again nudged the tire against his shin.

"Come on, say it!" the vampire taunted. He raised one arm from the handlebars and pushed Gabe roughly. "Say, 'I smell like a *pedo*.'"

Gabe staggered backwards. He winced when the chubby vampire rammed the bike against his knee. That hurt, and so did the slap on the side of his face. The punch in the arm—not really.

"You know what respect is? You know how to show it?"

The vampire suddenly lifted his eyes, as if he were watching the flight of a balloon released by a child. But there was no balloon, only a shadow, and the shadow had a thundering voice.

"What you doin'?" the voice boomed.

For a second, Gabe wondered if a third vampire had arrived to join the party. But when he turned, he recognized the brother he'd met near the Poverello House, the man who wore the sombrero. He was shirtless, ripped with muscle, and stern.

"I said, 'What you doin'?'" the brother asked the vampires. "Jacking up my friend?" He hooked a thumb at Gabe. "We go way back. Huh, amigo?"

[Gabe]

Gabe nodded like a bobble head.

The two vampires, straddling their bikes, had nothing to say. The air seemed to leak out of them. Slowly, they glided away, not bothering to look back.

"Ah, man," Gabe sighed. "Thanks. I mean it. Thanks."

"I see what's happenin'. Those *cholitos* be going to the grave early." The brother petted the puppy, smiled a golden smile, and informed Gabe he'd just had a marvelous piece of luck. He explained how a rich guy needed some muscle to clear out his three-car garage. He patted his pocket and said, "Got me eighty dollars and a pair of new socks." He pulled up his pant cuffs and shared the glow before continuing down the street.

Gabe hugged the puppy. He suddenly believed in miracles.

The puppy poked his nose in every corner of the living room. He climbed the recliner and the couch, and put his paws up on the coffee table. But when he began to gnaw on the leg of an end table, Gabe put a stop to his play. He cuddled the puppy next to his heart and christened him Lucky. He fed him a slice of lunch meat and placed a water bowl near the back door. When the eating and drinking were over, he gave the puppy a bath on the patio. He popped two ticks hiding in his scruff.

"Who's this?" asked his mother when she came home. She tossed her purse on an end table and frowned at the dog, then Gabe.

"Lucky," he answered. "Isn't he cool, Mom?" He reminded her that she had promised him a dog.

His mother groaned. She was too tired to argue. Instead, she kicked off her shoes and plopped down into the recliner. She threw her head back, closed her eyes for a few minutes, and then opened them. She smiled at the puppy.

"Where's he from?" she asked. "And when is he going back?"

"I found him in the street," Gabe answered. It was a small lie, he argued, the kind that would not darken his soul. He knew that he'd rescued the dog from a terrible fate. "You're joking, huh? I can keep him, huh?"

When Lucky wrestled a sock from under the couch, his mother smiled. "He's got talent," she had to admit. "He could be a search-and-rescue dog for dirty clothes."

Gabe beamed—he liked the tone of her giddiness.

"As long as he stays outside."

Gabe sprang from the couch and knelt next to his mother. He stroked her hair and patted her chubby hand.

"Mom, you're the best," Gabe cooed.

[Gabe]

She scooted up in the recliner, raising herself to a sitting position. "I saw your father today," she announced.

Gabe waited.

"He was over on Belmont," she added in a low voice. She played with the doily on the armrest then began to scrape absently a stain on her sleeve. She gazed up at Gabe. "A grown man pulling a suitcase. How pathetic."

Gabe was silent. Lucky had stopped chewing on the sock and sat up with his paws crossed. His tongue hung from his mouth.

"Mom," Gabe began. "He's sick. Let's take him in for a while."

"He wasn't very nice to us," she remarked without emotion.

Gabe couldn't offer an argument other than to say, "He's my dad."

"You're right about that." She petted Lucky and then remarked. "You can change husbands, but you can't change fathers."

Gabe could tell that his mother was rummaging through memories of their marriage. There had been plenty of bad days, but his dad had sometimes made her laugh, and he had sometimes surprised her with kindness. Once he had taken her up in a hot air balloon, where they drank champagne, she recalled, and dropped flowers and small candies on the party of friends below. It had been their fifth wedding anniversary, when Gabe, their love child, was six years old.

Gabe again asked about keeping the dog. He wanted to be sure that he had heard right.

"Yeah, you can keep him," she said wearily. "He *is* adorable."

Gabe leapt to his feet, sprinted into the kitchen, and fixed his mother a tall glass of iced tea. Next he went outside and picked mint from the side yard. Then he returned to the kitchen, sugared the tea with Sweet 'N Low, and presented the glass to her.

She sipped her drink, ran a hand through Gabe's hair, and said, "Gabriel Mendoza, you're a good son." She smiled at Lucky. When she snapped her fingers, he trotted over with a dirty sock in his mouth.

Gordo was not too pleased to have the puppy sniffing around, barking at the neighbor's dog, and raising a leg against the fence and clothesline. The cat hopped onto the fence rail and stood with his back turned to the two of them.

"Don't be like that, Gordo," Gabe begged. "He's only a puppy. Be nice." Gordo walked atop the fence and leapt down into the alley behind their house. He had been living the perfect life until Lucky showed up.

[Gabe]

Gabe made plans to sleep in the yard. He rolled out his sleeping bag, then hauled the ice chest from the garage and filled it with a treasure of ice. He arranged charcoal briquettes in the hibachi grill. After sunset, he would douse the briquettes with lighter fluid and throw a match on them.

"It's like camping," he told Lucky, who was gnawing at a flea roaming in his shoulder. The puppy scratched and scratched until Gordo reappeared, now on the neighbor's roof, his back still turned toward them. Lucky barked at Gordo, who, in turn, turned, hissed and showed his fangs.

Gabe's rations for the evening included soda, water, chips, and candy bars. He also had a bag of *chicharrones*. He had bowl of chilled grapes, too, and was eating a handful when his mother appeared in her pink slippers.

"It's cooler out here than inside," she remarked, her gaze rising to the neighbor's garage. "What's Gordo doing up there?"

"He's jealous," Gabe answered. "He's going to have to get used to Lucky."

Lucky climbed onto a plastic chair and placed his front paws on one arm, almost toppling it over. He again barked at Gordo until Gabe's mother removed him from the chair and sat down herself.

"He is cute," his mother said. "You used to be cute."

"I'm not anymore?"

"No, Gabe, you're not. Now you're handsome."

This compliment brought a smile to Gabe's face. He plunged his hand into the ice chest, the cold nearly hurting his heart, and brought out a bottle of water for his mother. She uncapped it, sipped and wagged a finger at Lucky, who was sniffing her slippers. "Don't even think about chewing them!"

Lucky, tail wagging, briefly let his tongue peek from his mouth.

"Yeah, he's a heartbreaker," his mother said and tickled his scruff. "The girl dogs are going to love him."

Gabe had finally seen happiness, and it had come in the shape of a dog. He was glad that he had risked a thumping from the Torres family. They didn't care for Lucky. In time, the law would knock on their front door.

"Did your father say he would come?" his mother asked.

In the late afternoon, Gabe had gone and found his dad at the library, head down on a table, sleeping. He'd invited him to come to the house at nightfall. He promised to roast hotdogs and cut open a watermelon.

"He said he would," Gabe answered. He pictured in his mind his father yawning and saying, "Ok, I'll be there."

"But he can't stay long. He can't sleep here, not even on the lawn."

[Gabe]

"He won't," Gabe promised. He sat down, cross-legged, on the sleeping bag. He admitted to himself that he wanted to see his dad. He was waiting for him. It would only be a short time before his dad unlatched the gate and entered the yard, dragging his years of toil.

"You know, we can't get back together," his mother reminded Gabe. She flipped off her pink slippers, then frowned at a blue vein on her thigh. "He's not a bad man. He's just a *borracho*." She examined the vein closely, not one bit happy about its bluish appearance.

After Gabe's mother went back into the house, Gabe and Lucky lounged together on the sleeping bag. Gordo disappeared from the roof, taking his jealousy elsewhere. Exhausted from the day, the dog lowered his head onto the grass and slept.

The night deepened like a bruise. The crickets began to sing, and the stars seemed to pulsate in the faraway heavens. A cool breeze rattled the pie tins.

Gabe reached for his T-shirt. He put the shirt on and woke up Lucky and pulled him into his lap. After a while, he struck a wooden match and tossed it on the coals, which flared and threw up wild flames. Startled, Lucky wriggled from Gabe's embrace, his tail pulled under his belly, scared.

"It's OK, Lucky. It's just a hibachi, a Japanese barbecue."

Lucky whined and barked.

Gabe watched the small grill and its glowing embers. To him, it was a signal of forgiveness. If his dad unlatched the back gate, he would find a son keeping a fire warm for him.

※

But his dad never came. The coals in the hibachi died, and something in Gabe's heart died as well. The next morning, he spread the coals in a flowerbed, like the ashes from a cremated body. His mother fumed, with anger shining in her eyes. At breakfast, she drank her coffee in big sips that produced wrinkles around her mouth. She told Gabe that his dad was a good-for-nothing, and threatened to call the cops if he ever came around.

"See! Your father can't keep his word!" she snapped, as if it were Gabe's fault. She tore open a package of Sweet 'N Low and poured its contents into a second cup of coffee.

Gabe stirred his soggy cereal, then spooned a single bite into his mouth. Nothing tasted good that morning. And his mother? Why was she always angry?

"Here you try to do something nice—and does he show up? No, he's too busy getting drunk or being stupid! The loser!" She set the coffee cup down and announced, "You're going to stay with one of your uncles." Gabe needed to get away, she said, for a

[Gabe]

week, if not longer, in case his father showed up with a basket of excuses.

Gabe didn't dare argue.

His mother stood up and told Gabe to clean the kitchen. She was late for work. She hugged her son and said, "Think about where you want to go— Uncle Jerry or Uncle Mathew." She swept the car keys off the counter and was gone.

Gabe was reluctant to stay with either uncle. If he left now, he would miss the last softball game of the season. Plus, there was Lucky. He was such a happy dog. His mother had promised to take care of him, even bring home high-end dog food. But she wanted Gabe gone from the house.

He chose Uncle Mathew, who lived on a vegetable farm in the foothills east of Fresno. Gabe packed his clothes and things into a cardboard box—nothing as fancy as a suitcase would please his uncle. His mother would take a few hours off from work to drive him there.

"Give it to me," his mother demanded, palm open, after they had gotten out of the car. Two chickens looked upon their arrival at Uncle Mathew's ranch.

"What?"

"Your phone."

"You don't really mean it."

"Yes, I mean it—give it to me."

Gabe reached into his back pocket. *Life without a phone!* How he was going to survive? Besides, he was worried about Lucky. The pup had just come into his life, and now his pup would be alone, for a week at least.

His mother didn't stay long, just enough time to drink a glass of cold lemonade and admire Uncle Mathew's vegetable garden, which covered nearly two acres. She left three wet kisses on Gabe's cheek and warned him to be a good boy.

Gabe knew he had to be good. His uncle was tough as beef jerky, and dark as jerky, too. The skin around his eyes was pleated from wincing at the sun. His teeth were yellow as candles, and his uncombed hair springy as wire.

"Gabe, you need to know what work is," Uncle Mathew told him on that first day, when he complained about the absence of his phone and Internet connection. You had to work to live under Uncle Mathew's roof.

Gabe was shown to a small room on the back porch, where his uncle stored cans of food, bags of rice and pinto beans, and paper sacks filled with walnuts and dried apricots, along with hammers, saws, drills, and any other tool that might rust if left in the barn.

"You'll survive," Uncle Mathew remarked, kicking a pile of overalls and soiled shirts into a

[Gabe]

corner. He unfolded a wooden cot and tossed a blanket and pillow onto it, then punched at the pillow.

"Thanks, Uncle," Gabe said weakly.

"Just like a fancy hotel," his uncle remarked snidely. "You got a view, too." He pointed at the yard, where chickens pecked at the sandy ground. "If you get hungry at night, you can help yourself to one of them. The hatchet's on the wall over there."

Gabe looked at the wall, where the hatchet hung at an angle. The blade did seem bloody red. Maybe his uncle wasn't joking.

The ranch was ninety miles east of Fresno, near Dinuba, above the smog line. The air was clear, and Gabe's responsibilities were equally clear. He had to work in the vegetable garden and do odd chores. His uncle lent him a wide-brimmed straw hat. He gave him a pair of worn leather gloves.

"You need to get your hands dirty," his uncle said, choosing a rasp that hung on the wall. He was fixing a table that he had scavenged from the roadside. "You got to know how to fix things, do things."

Gabe was braced for the lecture: kids had it made in Fresno, the city spoiled them, too many video games, too much music, blah, blah, blah.

"Don't make a face," his uncle ordered.

Gabe grinned.

"And don't grin either. Grinning is for pumpkins.

You a pumpkin?" His uncle turned to the damaged table. As he moved the rasp back and forth, little blond curls of wood fell to the floor.

After the first full day at Uncle Mathew's place, Gabe was second-guessing his decision. Maybe he should have gone to Uncle Jerry's instead. He was bored and exhausted. He figured that within a week he would be as tan as his uncle, with his face and neck dotted with mosquito bites.

They had worked all day shouldering splintery boards from the neighbor's barn. Uncle Mathew had asked if he could tear it down and salvage the wood. The watery-eyed farmer, who seemed to Gabe even older than the barn itself, had growled, "It's all yours. Don't sue me if it falls on your head."

Uncle Mathew intended to sell the wood for paneling. People from the city loved old barn-wood paneling. So, with a claw hammer, Gabe helped pry the boards from the collapsed frame and stack the lumber in the bed of the truck. They made three trips to the neighbor's farm. On the fourth, they gathered bent and rusty nails.

"Someone will buy these," his uncle said, holding one up. "They're collector items." He handed Gabe a steel rake and said, "See if you can find some more."

[Gabe]

Gabe did find more nails, but he also uncovered dead bats. Their faces were shrunken and their teeth small and yellowish.

That night Gabe heard coyotes howling in the distance. Wind rattled the galvanized roof and whistled through the windows, many of which were cracked and taped. His feet throbbed. How could this place be better than home?

"I'm tired," Gabe complained.

"Tired?" his uncle said. "Wait until tomorrow. Then you'll find out what tired means." His uncle had plans to dig a trench from the nearby creek to his garden patch.

On the fourth day, Gabe witnessed his uncle, hatchet in hand, corner a chicken. He covered his ears when the chicken screeched and leapt into the air, as if it could fly. He didn't have to ask his uncle what they were having for dinner.

Gabe could see how little his uncle had—the small plot of land, the meager crops, a few goats and chickens. To make ends meet, he rented a portion of the land to a woman who kept horses. He heard his uncle talk about her twice, and twice Gabe asked if he considered her pretty.

"Gabe," Uncle Mathew responded, "you sure are nosy."

One morning a truck swung into the yard, stirring up a cloud of dust. A woman got out of the cab and smiled through the haze. Gabe liked that, the first smiling person he had seen in days.

"Can you help me?" the woman asked, without introduction, as she walked around to the back of the truck, which was loaded with hay bales. She unchained the tailgate and let it fall.

Gabe had been digging at the stubborn roots of a dead tree, so he hurried to the truck and pulled out a bale. He carried it to the barn, surprised by its weight. He bumped a second bale with his knees, trying not to stagger and fall. He wanted to show the woman that he could do it.

On the way back for the third bale, Gabe tried to decode her license plate, which read, HTHERST. Heather's truck?

Uncle Mathew had come from behind the barn, where he had been sorting the lumber they had salvaged.

"Hi, Heather," Uncle Mathew greeted. There was music in his voice, a country twang. He hitched up his pants and pitched back his cowboy hat.

Who's grinning like a pumpkin now? Gabe asked himself. He likes her, for sure. When Gabe looked at Heather, he could see that the feeling was mutual—but why, Gabe couldn't understand. His uncle's hair was uncombed and he was wearing a funky-smelling work shirt that would scare away a skunk.

"Where's Corky?" his uncle asked, his smile turning to confusion. He looked into the cab of the truck.

[Gabe]

Heather shook her head and bit her lower lip. "I had to put him down. The vet said it was for the best." Her shoulders sloped noticeably.

Gabe thought of his own dog. He pictured Lucky sitting with one of his gym socks by the front door, waiting. Suddenly, Gabe missed him big time.

That afternoon Heather saddled two horses. One was for Gabe, who had never ridden a horse. As he swung one leg over the animal's back, Gabe was amazed at the feeling of a large living creature beneath him. He gripped the saddle's leather horn with both hands. The horse twisted its head, which was the size of a small duffle bag, and looked at him. Its large eyes were like mirrors; in their reflections Gabe could read the fear in his own face.

"Hold the reins lightly," Heather instructed. "I'll lead." She clicked her tongue and tapped the heels of her boots against her own horse's flanks.

Gabe's horse was named Moon Glow. The horse ambled in a way that made Gabe feel giddy, the jerky motion shaking his body from left to right. They climbed a hill and rode sometimes in the shade of trees, sometimes in the full blast of the afternoon sun. Gabe coaxed Moon Glow along by lightly shaking the reins. He was glad for his uncle's straw hat, and for his boots, too. The boots were large on his feet, but the heels could show the horse who was boss. Like Heather, he tapped his heels against the horse as they struggled across a granite ridge. The animal's hooves clicked against the granite, slipped, and rang.

"Careful, girl," Heather cooed.

Gabe was scared that the horse would topple over and land on him. He recalled the time Tomas Campo—the biggest kid in fourth grade—had tackled him in flag football. Tomas had driven the air from his lungs, leaving Gabe on the grass, gasping. The memory made him shudder.

"Good girl," Gabe sang, patting the horse's neck.

They rode in silence for a few more minutes, then Heather turned to Gabe and signaled for him to stop. "A rattler," she whispered.

Gabe looked where she was pointing and made out the rattlesnake half-hidden among leaves.

"Be still," Heather ordered. "He's just crossing."

Moon Glow took a single step backward. The snake showed its tongue, a little strip that reminded Gabe of the gum he used to pull from his mouth to see how long it would stretch. Its eyes were greenish and its head flat.

After the rattler finally slithered away, Gabe placed a hand on his racing heart.

Heather's destination was a small ridge that overlooked a dry terrain, large granite boulders and a mixture of oaks, willows, and evergreens. Hawks

[Gabe]

floated on the currents of warm air off the foothills. Lizards and rabbits darted from the brush. The sky was hazy, but the sun, angled in the west, was bright as a coin.

Gabe learned that Heather was a third-grade teacher. This piece of information made him squirm. He didn't tell her that the best things for him in that grade were recess, lunch, and more recess.

"Your uncle's a tough fella," Heather remarked. "But you know what he lacks?"

Gabe shrugged his shoulders and answered innocently, "A comb?"

Heather laughed. "No, Internet connection. Come on! Who lives without a computer? And with only a phone on the wall? Let's get real."

Gabe liked this third-grade teacher. He and Heather rested in the shade. Gabe drank from an old army surplus canteen. He splashed water against his face and rubbed some along the back of his neck. He examined his muddy palms then lay back, his hands behind his head, and closed his eyes.

"Penny for your thoughts," Heather asked.

"That's all—a penny?" He sat up.

"OK, a quarter."

Gabe became silent as he thought of Lucky. What was he doing at this very moment? Pulling socks from his drawer? Barking at Gordo their cat? Chewing on furniture?

"My dog," he answered.

"You have a dog?" Heather smiled and lifted the hair around her ears, as if she wanted to hear about a dog. "Let me guess—he's a pup, huh?"

"Me and Lucky—that's his name—were waiting for my dad," Gabe volunteered. He described the evening when he and Lucky had camped out in the backyard. How he had lit the hibachi, intending to grill hotdogs as a late-night snack. But did his dad come? No! His dad couldn't bother to show up!

Heather frowned sympathetically. "Your parents been divorced for a while?"

"Yeah, like years."

Gabe didn't want to see his father again. He was a bum and a liar. He was dead to him.

※

The next morning, Uncle Mathew shook him awake early. It was still dark when Gabe got dressed, drank a glass of milk, and stumbled outside. Moonlight gleamed against the walnut tree. The rooster seemed confused as Gabe moved toward the barn. His uncle ordered him to retrieve all the big containers he could find: boxes, wooden or cardboard, buckets and burlap sacks. They were going to raid their own vegetable garden and set up a roadside produce stand. They'd be selling corn, tomatoes, squash, chilies, eggplant, and walnuts—the cornucopia of plenty from the garden.

[Gabe]

"The early bird gets the longest, juiciest worm," his uncle remarked as he climbed into the truck. Gabe climbed in too then went back to sleep, hugging an old army blanket from the cold.

His uncle fiddled with the radio. It only worked if you banged it just right. When he couldn't find the country-western station he liked best, he snapped it off. He drove with his eyes on the road, the headlights cutting a path. The sky slowly began to pale into a new day. By the time they arrived at his uncle's favorite spot, the sun had come up beyond the grassy hills. He shook Gabe's shoulder. "Wake up, boy. We're here."

Under a fruitless mulberry tree, they set up two tables. Gabe spread newspaper on the tabletops then lugged over the boxes, buckets and burlap sacks. He taped up some old signs that were poorly drawn: the corn looked like a cigar and the tomatoes like rolled-up socks.

They were in the foothills. The only sounds were the thump of rabbits, the screech of an occasional hawk, and the hiss of crickets. Broken glass gleamed like diamonds at the edge of the road.

"Friday's a good day," his uncle said. Weekenders from Porterville and Visalia drove to the lake near Lemon Grove. They liked to stop at fruit stands, to feel like they were getting something right off the tree or a vine—and for a bargain.

"We got change?" Gabe asked.

"Glad you brought that up, boy." Uncle Mathew tapped the side of his head with a knuckle. "You'll need to use your noodle. If you're going to sell, you got to do the math right." He reached under the table and brought out a wrinkled paper bag of ones and fives and a large envelope of nickels, dimes, and quarters. He jingled the bag and said the sound of the coins was music to his ears.

"Now, I'm going away for a couple of hours," he said. He didn't offer an explanation. "When I return, I want the envelope a little heavier and these veggies mostly gone. Get what I mean? Be nice to the customers. Don't forget to say, 'Thank you.'"

His uncle disappeared, tires scattering gravel as the truck pulled onto the road. Gabe watched the truck turn the corner and disappear. Errands to do, he thought. Yeah, right. He was probably off to see Heather. Now and then Gabe would catch his uncle smiling as he worked—yeah, Gabe thought, he likes her a lot.

Gabe stood behind the table and watched as cars, RVs, and trucks pulling boats roared by. A few drivers glanced in his direction, but mostly they eyed the black road with determination, as if they were late for something. But late for what? The lake wasn't going anywhere.

When a van pulled up, Gabe wiped his hands on the front of his jeans. He smiled, eager for a sale—anything besides just standing there, bored.

[Gabe]

"Morning," Gabe greeted.

A man and his wife, both dressed in shirts bearing the American flag, ambled over to the tables. They eyed the produce. The man shooed a wasp from the pile of squash. The woman picked up two tomatoes and weighed them in her palm. Her shiny charm bracelet tinkled as she inspected the fruit.

The man chose an ear of corn and peeled back the husk. He placed it down again, wiping his hands against his pants. He squinted at the poorly drawn sign. "Four for a dollar," he mumbled. "That's not bad. OK, bag eight and some of those." He pointed at the squash set like grenades in a wooden box.

The couple made their purchases and drove away. Another car stopped, and then another. Some of the cars were loud with babies and kids, some had dogs that trotted off to raise a leg against a tree, bush, or rock. The envelope began to chime like a tambourine. The produce began to diminish. The tomatoes were gone first, followed by the corn. No one seemed to want walnuts until Gabe got the idea to crack open a few and eat them while the customers were mulling over what to buy. They would see Gabe snacking and say, "Give me a bag of those too."

Gabe was learning about people, and he was learning how to make a sale.

The sun arced across the sky. The day was

heating up. Flies buzzed around the dwindling stacks of produce.

After a last rush of customers, Gabe was left to himself, with only fruit flies for company. Then he detected a shadow behind him. He spun around to face a man staring at him. For a brief moment, Gabe thought, *How did dad get here?*

"Hello, son," the man mumbled, without much energy. He looked homeless—was homeless.

Gabe grew suspicious at his use of the word "son." Who was this guy?

The stranger stepped toward the table.

Gabe asked, not unkindly, "You want something, mister?"

The man placed his blackened, root-like fingers on the edge of the table, mouthed an unintelligible word, and gazed at the produce. He picked up the last bunch of baby carrots, and then a single squash. He took a walnut into his hand and then set it back down like a chess piece.

Gabe was sure the man was a drifter, with no place to call home. His bed would be a patch of grass, a sheet of cardboard, a discarded mattress, or a dirty blanket around his shoulders. He was closer to dust than any man Gabe had ever seen.

"You want something to eat?"

A tear shone in the stranger's eye.

"I gotta sandwich," Gabe offered. "It's just cheese and tomato. But I got some crackers, too."

[Gabe]

"That would be nice," the man answered plainly.

The two ate standing next to the tables, the former site of plenty.

Gabe stood on the front porch, shirtless. Wind raked the corn patch, rattling the leaves. A coyote behind the oak trees howled. Lightning flashed in the east. Gabe made exploding sounds.

"Give it a rest," his uncle suggested. He was shaving the insulation from a length of copper wire. The wire, he explained, was as good as gold—no, it was even better because it was attainable. He had found the large spool of copper wire in an old truck with its nose in a ditch. Trucks and cars, some with bullet holes in their windshields, were abandoned throughout the valley.

Earlier in the day the heavy air sagged around them. Now a warm wind stirred the garden and forced the galvanized roof to lift and dance. The chickens in the barn squawked after each flash of lightning. The horses in the far pasture neighed.

"Get over here and help," his uncle ordered.

Gabe did as he was told. He sat on an overturned bucket and began stripping insulation from the wire. They worked in silence. Since Gabe's fingers were nimble, not work-worn like his uncle's, he was able to strip off the insulation more quickly.

While his uncle grumbled, Gabe whistled. This was easy. Had he discovered his calling in life?

"How's your mom?" his uncle asked.

Gabe wasn't sure how to describe his everyday life in Fresno. He replied, "OK, I guess."

"She like her job?"

"No."

"Glad to hear that. Shows she's smart upstairs." Uncle Mathew tapped his temple and then paused before he said, "She told me you saw your father."

Gabe nodded.

Uncle Mathew waited for Gabe to add to the story. When Gabe didn't reply, his uncle remarked, "Families can be messed up, including ours. Or should I say, especially ours."

Lightning cut across the sky like scissors. It outlined the trees and momentarily brought the rows of corn out of darkness. Thunder rolled through the air.

Gabe risked asking, "Uncle, how did you end up living here?"

"Sounds like you think this is the end of the world."

No television, no Internet, no phone—yeah, for Gabe it *was* the end of the world.

"You know what I mean."

"Yeah, I know what you mean." He inhaled and exhaled the truth. "I was married—twice."

"Twice! No way," Gabe hollered. But his

[Gabe]

exclamation was lost in another roll of thunder.

"Yeah, and to good women," his uncle confided. He told Gabe how he fell in love with wife number one when he was in the army and stationed in Germany. There, he had been assigned to a parachute battalion.

"That's way cool!" Gabe crowed. He liked jumping from heights, trees and rooftops mostly. But that was kid stuff. What could be better than jumping from a plane, with the wind rushing past your ears until the parachute opened and rocked you slowly to earth?

"Cool? More like scary. Nearly pooped my pants the first time. "

Uncle Mathew looked in the distance as a lightning strike lit up the hills. His thoughts continued far beyond the horizon to another side of the world. "But I messed up. I was drinking every night. I was stupid, unfaithful, loud, always loud and arguing over nothing."

The story stopped there. He told Gabe to get them some lemonade, and to hurry up about it.

"I'm on it," Gabe said, jumping to this feet. But when he returned from the kitchen, his uncle had left the porch. He was out in the yard, a lone figure. The lightning cut across the sky. For a second the outline of his uncle seemed to light up before he was thrown back into the dark.

Poor Uncle, Gabe thought. He had chased away his first wife. Knowing that, Gabe couldn't imagine what had happened to the second wife. Marriage, he was learning, was complicated. He only had to think of his mother and his father—or a lot of his classmates with divorced parents. Few families stuck together.

The night crackled. The wind blew hot. The leaves of the corn rustled, and the chickens squawked in fear.

Gabe's uncle dropped him off at home two days later, without bothering to stop and visit with his sister. He was having trouble with the truck's alternator—the battery wouldn't store power. He patted Gabe's shoulder and said, "Too bad you won't be around tonight."

"Why?" Gabe asked, holding a cardboard box in his arms.

"Because I'm gonna introduce one of the chickens to my hatchet!" His uncle's yellowish teeth glowed as he laughed.

Gabe pictured a chicken scattering as his uncle tiptoed toward that feathered creature with a murderous gleam in his eye. "That's not even funny."

"Not for the chicken!" Uncle Mathew chuckled, shifted into first gear, and drove away. The exhaust pipe popped and the tools in the back of the truck clanged.

[Gabe]

Gordo was on the front lawn, paws pressed together, sitting as still as a statue. As Gabe stroked his head, the chrome bell under the cat's chin made a tinkling sound.

"How's the barrio?" Gabe asked.

The cat meowed, but didn't move a whisker. He blinked sleepily.

When Gabe pushed open the front door, he discovered a heavyset man on the couch. For a second, Gabe feared that he had entered the wrong house. But there was the owl-shaped clock, whose tail beat time to the seconds, and the family photos in their wooden frames on the wall. Plus, there was no mistaking the Raiders blanket on the couch—that was his for sure.

"Hi," the man said in a low, husky voice, not bothering to rise. He was lacing up a shoe. Gabe could see a bald spot near the back of the man's head. The skin was pink. He was a man who worked indoors, maybe mom's coworker at Walmart?

Gabe glanced at the man—could he be his mother's boyfriend?—then headed straight to his bedroom. Right away, he recognized his rudeness. He should have offered at least a "Hi" in return. A few minutes later, he heard the front door open. There was a pause, the door closed, and then his mother's footsteps came padding over the carpet toward his bedroom. She knocked and entered.

"Gabe," she said brightly, "you're so tan!" When

she gave him a hug, he offered a polite squeeze. He could smell the perfume on her. "Tell me, how was it?" Her eyes took him in from head to toe. "And look at you! Didn't Uncle feed you?"

"Yeah, mainly *frijoles*."

"Great! That's what we're having tonight!" his mother joked.

She led him to the living room. Be cool, he warned himself. He could feel his mother's happiness. Why not return the happiness? His mother had to have someone in her life, so why not the portly dude on the couch?

Gabe's mother read his thoughts. "You're wondering who that guy was."

"Yeah," Gabe admitted. "Is he your boyfriend?" It felt strange saying "boyfriend." His mother had dated a couple of times since his father's departure, but it had been years since he'd seen her with another man.

"He might be," she answered girlishly. "We'll see."

But Gabe could see that he was her boyfriend. She had a smile on her face and she seemed shapelier. Had she lost a few pounds in the ten days since he'd been gone? Her hair was combed, her lips red with lipstick. She was dolled up, for sure.

In the kitchen, his mother made him a strawberry smoothie.

"Mom," Gabe began. "Uncle Mathew is old

[Gabe]

school. He works really hard." He told her about the broken-down barn that he had helped dismantle, about the hours he had spent battling bees and wasps in the garden, the roadside fruit stand, the copper wire, the trench he dug, and his first horse ride. But he stopped talking when Lucky trotted into the living room. The pup had grown. Instead of prancing awkwardly over his floppy feet, he was coordinated now.

"Lucky!" Gabe cried, falling to his knees. Lucky leaped into his arms and began to mop Gabe's face with his tongue. After this brief reunion, his mother informed him that a boy had come by asking for him.

"What boy?" Gabe's mood changed from giddiness to worry.

"I don't know," she answered. "I was in the front yard watering. He was with some other boys."

Frankie, Gabe thought.

"He said that you owe him something." With a sour look on her face, she told Gabe how he had spit when he left. "Such a *mocoso,* a little snot."

"He spit at you?"

"Not at me, at the ground. Still, I didn't like it."

Gabe was on full alert now. He would have to deal with Frankie. He rose, lifting the T-shirt off his body. "I'm going to take a shower" he said. He left the kitchen, with Lucky following him to the bathroom.

"What are you going to do?" he asked the dog. "Get in the shower with me?"

Lucky put his paws on the edge of the tub, but Gabe removed them. He climbed into the shower, screaming from the blast of cold water. He turned clockwise, then counter clockwise, and felt happy to be home. When he got out of the shower, he noticed beads of water hanging from Lucky's jaws.

"You been drinking out of the toilet?"

The dog barked *Yes*.

Gabe learned that his dad had come around, just as his mother predicted. One early evening, he had knocked on the front door and called Gabe's mother's name, then Gabe's name. But his mother wouldn't open the peephole and look. No, she was done with him. How dare he stand up *her* son! What kind of man was he?

Gabe learned this over a dinner of enchiladas, *arroz*, and *frijoles*—his first good meal in a week. He only ate one serving, however, and turned down the soda his mother offered. Instead, his beverage was sugarless iced tea.

Gabe conjured up an image of the man on the couch. "Do you really like him?" Gabe asked his mother.

"He's nice," she answered. "He's not real pretty,

[Gabe]

but he's kind and he's got a job." She sipped her iced tea, one eye on Gabe, then said, "Pass the tortillas."

Gabe knew this meant the subject was finished for the moment. He helped with the dishes and then went outside, leaving Lucky behind. He couldn't risk parading his puppy through the neighborhood. Someone would say, "Yeah, I saw the dog. Gabe's got him."

He decided he would risk Holmes Playground, even though it was already getting dark. Gabe was eager to seek advice from Coach Rodriguez about how to handle Frankie. Plus, he wanted to apologize for skipping the last game of the season.

Gabe learned that Coach Rodriguez would be gone the entire week—vacation time in Santa Cruz. He asked about the last softball game and was told that his team had won, 7-3, against Pinedale. He felt good about the win.

Gabe slipped out of the playground. He walked two blocks in the direction of a strip mall, intending to buy himself a bag of sunflower seeds. But he halted along the way, like a fox sensing danger. Up ahead, Frankie and his crew were in front of the 7-Eleven. One of them was sneaking a glance into a parked car, looking to break a window and steal whatever was in the backseat.

"You ain't sly," Gabe whispered as he waited for a traffic light to turn green. "You think people can't see you? They can see you."

Gabe hesitated before he crossed the street, thinking that he might as well have it out with Frankie. In time, Frankie would track him down anyway. Why not throw punches tonight? He moved quickly through the strip mall, his head down, knowing he would be instantly on Frankie's radar.

"Hey, fool!" Frankie yelled.

Gabe didn't respond. He entered the 7-Eleven, where the bright fluorescent lights made him squint. He stood still as his eyes adjusted, then gazed at the pudgy cashier, a Middle Eastern man, whose beard was smoky gray. Gabe walked causally over to the racks of candies and picked up a Butterfinger, weighed it in his palm, then set it back down. He sauntered down an aisle where the sunflower seeds hung among the potato chips. From there, he could spy Frankie and his crew huddled together. Although they were only wannabe homies, they were dangerous in their own way.

"Just do it," Gabe ordered himself.

He exited the 7-Eleven without making a purchase, marched over to Frankie, and smacked him in the jaw. Frankie was rocked. His hands rose immediately, covering his face as if in prayer, when Gabe hit him a second time.

"How come you spit at my mom?" Gabe shouted. He wasn't sure if Frankie had spit at his mother, but his roar was real. No one would fault a son for defending his mother.

[Gabe]

When one of Frankie's crew flew at him, Gabe reached for the collar of his T-shirt and pulled him to the ground. But the homie, scrambling to his knees, grabbed Gabe's leg and bit his calf. Gabe jerked his leg away as teeth raked against his skin. The homie let go, his chin scraping the asphalt. The homie yelped from pain.

Gabe growled when the smallest crewmember climbed onto his back. He spun, trying to shake him off. But the homie wouldn't let go and even managed a few weak karate chops to the back of his neck. Finally, Gabe managed to throw him off by thrusting an elbow into his gut.

The homie groaned. He hugged his stomach, the air knocked out of him.

"Oops, my bad!" Gabe hollered. He lowered his shoulder and rammed him like a linebacker. The homie dropped, still holding his stomach, his legs bicycling like a smashed spider.

Gabe's eyes flashed rage at Frankie. "What did you call me? A fool? Look at your loser friend on the ground. I'm gonna put you there too!" When Gabe raised a fist, Frankie, eyes leaking, backed up. Gabe couldn't tell whether they were crybaby tears or tears of pain.

"I'm gonna get you," Frankie cried, his mouth twisted with anger.

Gabe slapped him. "You gonna do what?"

Frankie put his hand up to the side of his face.

He grimaced but didn't fight back. Snot ran from his nose. His eyes became wet with tears.

"Three of you, one of me!" Gabe roared. "You guys are weak."

The homie that had been on the ground, holding his stomach, was now on his feet. He didn't want any more of Gabe.

The crew backed up, done for the moment, and ran to the street corner. They looked back. The smallest homie gave Gabe the finger. The other spit and yelled, "I know where you live."

"Come by anytime," Gabe yelled. "I'll mow my front lawn with your ugly face!" Gabe couldn't help but imagine the kid as a lawn mower, his teeth chewing off blades of grass.

When Gabe got to the house, his mom was gone—a note left on the coffee table read that she would be back by ten o'clock. He showered a second time for the day, soaping his body carefully. He probed the back of his neck, where several blows had landed. He touched his bruised ribs. He examined his calf and ankle.

"Dang," he muttered. The homie actually had bitten through his skin, leaving two puncture holes. "Punk vampire."

Afterwards, his hair still damp, he called Uncle Mathew.

[Gabe]

"You woke me up," he complained groggily.

Gabe raised his eyes to the clock on the wall: 9:37pm. He remembered his uncle's habit of going to bed early. I sleep when the chickens sleep, he'd joked.

"Sorry I woke you," Gabe said. "I need Heather's number."

"What, you got a crush on her?" his uncle asked, then chuckled. Gabe could hear the bedsprings groan as his uncle sat up.

"Uncle, I got a problem." Gabe tried to explain the situation, his right hand rolling automatically into a fist as he described the parking-lot scuffle.

"Give me a break! Home one day and already in trouble?" He sighed heavily, then growled, "OK, wait a minute. Let me get her number."

After reading out the number, he told Gabe to be careful. He could come and live on the ranch if he wanted. Just today, he uncle said, he'd sold the lumber from the old barn.

"That's great," Gabe said, imagining the dollar bills he kept in a jar hidden on the back porch. "I may have to come live with you. We'll see."

"That would be all right with me," Uncle Mathew replied. He yawned, then followed up with an angry outburst about the alternator he'd had to replace in the truck.

"Cost me seventy-eight bucks for a used one. And I had to drive all the way to Visalia to get it."

Gabe listened patiently to his uncle complain about the long drive, then thanked him and apologized for calling so late. He hung up and dialed Heather. He left his number on her voicemail. Seconds later, she called back.

"Gabe?" Heather asked.

"I got a problem," Gabe said for the second time that night. He told Heather about the showdown with Frankie and his crew. He described the bites around is ankle.

"Violence won't get you anywhere," Heather responded.

"I'm not violent," Gabe argued. He pointed in the direction of Frankie's house, six blocks away. "It's him, it's his whole stupid family." Then he told her the real reason why he wanted to speak to her. "I know your dog just died. I'm calling to see if you would take Lucky."

"I don't know, Gabe," Heather responded after a moment of silence.

"They're gonna come and take Lucky—I know they will. They're gonna make him fight."

He and Heather went back and forth until she finally melted. "Actually, I'll be in Fresno the day after tomorrow. I'll pick up Lucky then."

Gabe squeezed his eyes closed in gratitude.

"What if I call you when I get into town? It'll be around four."

Gabe gave Heather his street address. He told

[Gabe]

her she was really nice and added, "You know, Uncle Mathew likes you."

She giggled and said, "Of course he does. All little doggies like me." She hung up before Gabe could say that his uncle *really* liked her.

Gabe glowed at the possibility that Heather might also like his uncle. True, he was dirty from work most of the time, but he was trustworthy. His uncle wouldn't mess up a third marriage—this, Gabe was sure about.

He returned to the kitchen, opened the refrigerator for a handful of sliced bologna, and then went outside.

"Lucky," Gabe called as he walked into the yard. "I got a treat for you."

Gabe had chained Lucky to the clothesline, but he was gone—chain and all. *Frankie*, he growled to himself. He looked around frantically, then peered over the fence into the dark alley.

His dog was gone, stolen, kidnapped—whatever! Dejected, he sat on a rickety plastic chair and put a slice of bologna into his mouth. He was going to need all the strength to get his dog back.

When his mother came home at 10:17, Gabe was on the couch, feeling more like a parent than a teenager.

"I would say that you're busted, Mom." He lifted his eyes at the clock, indicating that she was seventeen minutes late. The first rush of anger about losing Lucky had run through his veins. He was emotionally depleted. Now he was more relaxed as he had plans for rescuing Lucky a second time.

"You're worse than me." She was wearing a dress—not the usual jeans and T-shirt—and adorned with a bead necklace and a copper-colored bracelet. The scent of perfume surrounded her.

"What's his name again?" Gabe asked. He figured that he had every right to pry. He didn't want his mom dating just anybody.

His mother stood in front of the hallway mirror. She ignored his question as she took off her jewelry and checked her lipstick in silence. "His name is Bobby," she finally answered when she pulled away from the mirror.

"He looks OK," Gabe agreed.

"A little fat, but who isn't?" His mother touched her own stomach.

"You said he has a job. What does he do?"

"Risk management."

Gabe didn't bother to ask what that meant. As long as he had a job, he was an all right guy.

"I'm off to bed," his mother announced, dismounting from her platform shoes. "Dating makes me so tired."

After his mother vanished into the bathroom,

[Gabe]

Gabe made his way to his bedroom. He plopped down on his bed, hands folded over his stomach, and waited for his mother to finish up in the bathroom. Finally, his mother called, "Good night, Gabe," and he yelled, "Goodnight, Mom." When he was certain that she was in bed, he put on his shoes, changed into a dark T-shirt, and climbed out his bedroom window.

Along the way dogs barked at Gabe. But as soon as he passed, they quieted down. He stopped at the end of Frankie's block. He could see cop cars, their lights spinning and shining up into the trees. The neighborhood residents stood on the sidewalk or in the street. Some of them were in pajamas, others half-dressed in jeans or baggy sweats, excited by the commotion.

At first, Gabe thought there must have been a fire. But he didn't smell smoke or see any fire engines.

"They got busted," he realized. He recalled the stacks of groceries in the garage, and imagined stolen phones, video games, and laptops inside the house. A friend must have snitched—or someone with a grudge called the police on them. Why not? They were no good!

Gabe ventured toward the crowd. He spotted Frankie and Tony and their parents on the front lawn. The father, shirtless and displaying tattoos on arms and belly, was handcuffed. He had grass in his hair, as if he had been wrestling with one of the cops in a futile attempt at an escape.

Because the action was in front of the house, Gabe didn't think he would be noticed if he moved to rescue Lucky. He sprinted around the block and into the alley. He peeked through the slats of the tall redwood fence: no cops, no family members and no Lucky. When he found the gate latch locked, he boosted himself over the fence. As he plopped silently into the yard, the safety light came on.

Gabe jumped into the shadow of the garage. He could hear the squawk of a radio from a patrol car and the voice of one of the cops out front. He glanced around the backyard—junky car parts, old tires, plastic bags of recycled bottles, an overturned barbecue with its legs in the air, a deflated blow-up swimming pool, a parched garden—but no Lucky. Then Gabe heard a single bark from inside the house. He pushed himself away from the garage and peeked into a bedroom window: Lucky was playing with a sock.

Gabe's mind whirled. He decided that he would just walk in and claim the dog. After all, the father was handcuffed in the front. What could they do?

Gabe crept to the kitchen door. He touched the doorknob with a single finger first, as if it might be hot, then his whole hand wrapped around the knob. He opened the door, peeked inside and, seeing no one, let himself in. He tiptoed through the kitchen—dirty dishes piled high in the sink—and paused before passing the living room—no one was seated

[Gabe]

on their messy couch. He sped to the back bedroom.

When Gabe entered the bedroom, he encountered a large cop going through the contents of a cardboard box. The cop slowly raised his face from the box. His rough expression said: What do you want? His even rougher voice boomed, "You're not supposed to be here!"

Gabe took in everything about the cop: the two stripes on his sleeves, the holstered gun, the mace and handcuffs, the row of bullets attached to his belt, and the thick-soled shoes—one was scuffed, the other shiny. Gabe considered backtracking, but he stood his ground. He and the cop looked at each other, like David and Goliath.

Finally, the cop barked, "Did you hear me? You're supposed to be outside."

"My dog," Gabe replied. "Let me get him." Gabe figured the cop would think that he was just one of the unfortunate sons of the man handcuffed on the front lawn. What's the big deal? Let the boy have the pup, Gabe hoped the cop was thinking.

The cop jerked his head at Lucky. Go head, the gesture said, take him. The cop returned to examining the box.

Lucky was already standing up, tail wagging. When Gabe called him, the pooch ran into his arms.

At home, Gabe drank from the garden hose in the backyard, then held out the hose for Lucky to drink. Water splashed off the dog's snout.

"You're a brave dog," Gabe told Lucky. He threw himself on the front lawn, and Lucky leaped onto him, nosing his neck until Gabe laughed uncontrollably. He quieted, though. His mother's bedroom faced the lawn.

Gabe figured it all out: Frankie would find the dog gone and blame the police—a door was left open, and Lucky trotted off to freedom. Gabe would just have to keep him off the streets until Heather came. And that would be easy. He would hunker down and watch television, play video games, and do chores for his mother. He would be a very good son.

In the darkness of the yard, Gabe watched the sky. He counted two shooting stars within minutes of each other. When the cold began to seep through his body, he rose, brushed the grass from his pants, and boosted Lucky through his bedroom window.

The next morning, Gabe grubbed on soy *chorizo* with Egg Beaters, a brand of imitation egg. He could see that his mother had become serious about losing weight. Was it because of the new man in her life? He would ask more about Bobby in time. For now, he praised his mom's cooking. He tore a piece of tortilla and pinched up some fake egg.

A few minutes after his mother left for work, Uncle Mathew called from a payphone, asking

[Gabe]

Gabe if he was OK.

"Everything's cool," Gabe answered.

"Did you get in touch with Heather?"

The real reason for the call, Gabe figured. At that time of day, Uncle would have already spent a couple of hours in the garden or in the barn. Sweat would have lathered the hair under his cowboy hat.

"Yeah, she's coming to get Lucky."

"Who?"

"Lucky. I told you about him. She's going to take him." Gabe lacked the energy to explain how Lucky had been nabbed. Instead, he said, "I think she likes you."

"What? Who likes me? The dog?"

"You heard me. Heather, she likes you. And you like her!" Gabe had to smile at the crazy idea of Uncle Mathew in love!

"You're such a little liar."

"She said that you have bazookas for arms." Gabe willed himself not to laugh.

"Don't be funny, boy!" warned Uncle Mathew. He told Gabe that he would make a good Cupid, and then he hung up.

With Lucky at his side, he went to the garage. Gabe didn't relish cutting the front lawn in the heat, but he promised his mom. It wasn't so scraggly as to be an embarrassment on an otherwise tidy street. Still, he shut Lucky in the backyard, then had the mower on the lawn when Pablo rode past on his new bike.

Pablo saw him and circled back.

"Hey," said Gabe, walking out to meet his friend.

"Did you hear about Frankie's dad?" Pablo straddled his bike. He was breathing hard.

Gabe feigned ignorance.

"He had all this stolen stuff, Nikes and Hollister shirts, computers, phones, even drones—man, I got to get me a drone." Pablo raised a hand over his head to show how high the contraband was piled. "Now he's got a bus ticket to Happy Valley Prison."

Pablo rode away, neither hand on the handlebars, the sort of balancing act that was a cinch for a jock like him. He said he was off to Holmes Playground to see about the start of soccer season.

This was the best news since the beginning of time—Frankie and his family moving away! Gabe sprinted into the backyard and whistled to Lucky, who was pawing at a deflated soccer ball. With Lucky leading the way, the two climbed the stairs and went inside house. Gabe called Heather on the landline telephone. She picked up on the third ring.

"Heather, it's me," he began. "I have something to tell you." Gabe figured that if Frankie was gone—out of the neighborhood, out of his life—he could keep Lucky for himself. Heather would understand. She had owned dogs before and would know the pain of giving up a dog.

"And what is that?" Heather's voice was light, full of happiness.

[Gabe]

"You know that boy who was messing with me? The one who stole Lucky?" He explained why the Torres family was moving away. "Heather, if it's OK with you, can I keep Lucky? Is it OK?" He felt guilty about retracting his offer.

"Of course."

"You're not mad?"

"No, I have a new dog. He's not house trained yet, but he will be." She chuckled and added, "He needs a flea bath, too."

Gabe looked at the clock on the wall. Uncle Mathew was already at her place! It had been—what?—less than forty minutes since they'd spoken on the phone? For the sake of romance, he hoped that Uncle Mathew had at least brushed his teeth and changed his shirt.

After he hung up, Gabe went back outside, chained Lucky to the clothesline, and made his way over to Frankie's house to see for himself. The last van was leaving, a heavyset guy at the wheel. The van rode over the curb, springs squeaking, and slowly drove away.

Gone for good! Gabe could have danced in the street. Instead, he started walking towards Chinatown, in spite of the heat, then hopped onto a bus, grateful for the air conditioning. After a two-mile ride, he got off the bus, a blast of warm exhaust overwhelming him as it pulled away. He strolled past a few stores—only Central Fish was bringing in customers—and crossed Ventura Avenue. If his dad was anywhere, it would be near the Poverello House—or a homeless camp near Highway 99.

Gabe ghosted through the area for an hour before boarding a bus on Tulare Street. He took a seat in the back. Now that he was sitting still, he began to sweat even more. All his energy had been used in trekking to a part of town his mother had warned him against.

At a red light, Gabe glanced out the bus window and saw a man bent over a city trash bin chained to a lamppost. He was pulling out plastic bottles and aluminum cans: garbage to some, treasure to others. His clothes seemed to have been dragged through a dusty field. He wore no socks. His shoelaces were undone.

Gabe felt sorry for this person. At least it's not my dad, he told himself. But when the man turned—the bus was beginning to move—he saw that it was his dad. He was holding up two plastic bottles, shaking out their contents—drops of liquid falling like tears on the hot cement.

When school started, Gabe and Pablo joined a soccer team called the Renegades. One Saturday, after an away game, the team stopped at a supermarket. Still in cleats, they strolled through

[Gabe]

the supermarket. Gabe went in search of beef jerky, his favorite snack. Then, to offset the salty treat, he made his way to the produce section for something sweet but healthy. To his surprise, his dad was at a produce island, building a pyramid of oranges. His busy hands looked like the hands of a magician as he juggled the oranges and put them in order. He then looked up.

"Gabe!" his dad called, eyes gleaming with excitement. Smiling widely, he came around the island. He took Gabe's shoulders in his hands and gave them a friendly shake. Now they stood together, son and father.

"You playing soccer?" his dad asked. He gazed down at the shin guards and cleats. "And look at you, you've grown taller."

That was true. In a year or so, he would surpass his dad in height. He tried not to remember that figure of a man bending over a trash bin. He tried to focus on where his dad stood now, a man with a job. On his belt, he carried a small holster with a pruning knife and a box cutter. He wore an apron and a nametag that read Ronald Mendoza. Perhaps he was someone after all.

"I got my act together," his dad said in a low voice. "Got some job training, then a friend from high school—he's the manager here—hired me." He shrugged his shoulders. "It's a job, it's something. And I get all the veggies and fruit I want!"

Gabe listened to his dad for a few more minutes, then politely said, "Dad, I got to go. They're waiting." He backed away, the cleats clacking against the floor.

"I'll give you a call," his dad said. He pulled out a phone. "I got one like everybody else." He asked for Gabe's number.

Gabe hesitated as his gaze turned to the pyramid of oranges. At least his dad could do that right, arrange fruit in an orderly pile.

"OK," Gabe said. As he gave his number, he noticed his dad's Adam's apple riding up and down, a sign that he was hurting inside, that the moment was emotional for him.

Outside the market, a rush of cool autumn air greeted him. Coach was waving him over to the van, waving for him to hurry. The door was open and his teammates were jostling each other. One of them was spinning a soccer ball on a finger. Another was bouncing one off his knee.

But would he? Would he call his dad? A lump of sadness thickened in his throat. Tears invaded his eyes. He gazed back at the supermarket. His dad was inside, doing a job any teenager could do. But it was a job, it was a paycheck, it was somewhere to be.

"My poor Dad," Gabe found himself whispering. If his dad called, Gabe decided that he would be nice. He would give him another chance. Everyone

[Gabe]

needs a second—or third—chance, just like Uncle Mathew, who was engaged to marry Heather.

"Let's go, Gabe!" the coach called. He was holding a giant pretzel in one hand, a juice drink in the other. "We've been waiting for you."

Waiting for you.

Gabe thought that maybe his dad had been waiting too, hoping for years when he could abandon his street life, clean up his act and bring a forgotten son into his arms.

"I'm there, Coach," Gabe yelled. He slipped his phone into his waistband, skipped and hustled to the idling van.

Gary Soto

Gary Soto began writing poetry in the early 1970s. Since then, he as published more than thirty books, including *Sudden Loss of Dignity*, *The Spark and Fire of It: A Romance*, and *F. Pérez Lopez's El Mexicano*, titles available from Stephen F. Austin State University Press. He is author of *In and Out of Shadows*, a musical about undocumented youth. He lives in Berkeley, California.

CPSIA information can be obtained
at www.ICGtesting.com
Printed in the USA
FFHW020416150219
50550341-55860FF